Disney

Tales of
MAGIC

This Edition Exclusive to:

(949) 587-9207

Produced and published by
INNOVAGE, Inc.
19511 Pauling
Foothill Ranch, CA
92610
Tel: (949) 587-9207
Fax: (949) 587-9024

Printed in CHINA

CONTENTS

Walt Disney's DUMBO

It was spring, spring in the circus!

After the long winter's rest, it was time to set out again on the open road, and everyone was eager to go.

"Toot! Toot!" whistled Casey Junior, the locomotive of the circus train.

"All aboard!" shouted the Ringmaster.

The acrobats, the jugglers, the tumblers, and the snake charmers scrambled to their places on the train. The keepers locked the animal cages. Then with a jiggedy jerk and a brisk puff-puff, off sped Casey Junior. The circus was on its way!

Everyone was singing. Everyone was happy. All the mother animals had new babies to love. All but Mrs. Jumbo. Her baby elephant had not yet arrived, and she wondered how the stork would ever find her.

But what was this?

A special-delivery stork was flying pell-mell after the circus train.

"**M**rs. Jumbo? Where is Mrs. Jumbo?" he asked the two giraffes.

Eventually, the stork found the elephant car and left his precious bundle at Mrs. Jumbo's side.

All the other elephants were waiting to see the new baby. And what a darling, chubby baby elephant he was. "This is a proud day for us elephants," said one of the grown-ups to Mrs. Jumbo, and she tickled the baby under his chin. "Koochie koo, little Jumbo, koochie koo!

The tickling made him sneeze. And when he sneezed, out flapped his ears—enormous ears! The biggest ears any elephant had ever seen! "He'll never be a little Jumbo," laughed the grown-ups. "Little Dumbo is the name for him!"

Poor little Dumbo toddled to his mother, and tenderly, she rocked him to sleep in her trunk.

Before morning dawned, Casey Junior brought the train to a stop in the city where the circus was to open that day. As soon as the tents were all set up, the circus folk got ready for the big parade. Down the main street pranced the gay procession. There were cream-white horses and licorice-colored seals. There were lady acrobats in pink silk tights, lions pacing in their gilded wagon-cages, and last but not least came the elephants marching slowly, in single file.

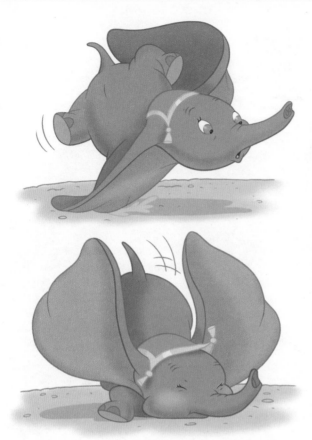

At the end of the line came little Dumbo, and all went well until the crowd caught sight of him. "Look at that silly animal with the draggy ears!" they cried. "He can't be an elephant! He must be a clown!" Dumbo, toddling along behind his mother with his trunk clasped around her tail, tried to hurry faster so he wouldn't hear the laughter.

But alas, he stumbled and tripped on his ears. Down he went in a puddle of mud. The crowd roared with laughter at the baby elephant.

Back in the tent, Mrs. Jumbo gave Dumbo a bath so that he would look fine for the first show that afternoon. When she had carefully wrung out his ears and Dumbo had shaken himself dry, they ate their lunch and then went to their stalls in the menagerie.

Soon the crowd was streaming through the tents. A group of boys gathered near the rope in front of Mrs. Jumbo's stall. "We want to see the baby elephant!" they yelled. "The one with the sailboat ears!

Look, there he is." A boy grabbed one of Dumbo's ears and pulled it, hard. Then he made an ugly face and stuck out his tongue.

Mrs. Jumbo could not stand to see Dumbo being teased. She reached out with her trunk, snatched the boy up, dropped him across the rope, and spanked him. "Help, help!" he cried.

"**W**ild elephant!" someone else shouted. And then the keepers came running. Mrs. Jumbo reared on her hind legs.

But soon she was behind the bars in the prison wagon with
a big sign above her that said
"Danger! Mad elephant! Keep out!"

Worst of all, the other elephants would
have nothing to do with Dumbo.
"He's a disgrace to elephants all over
the world," they said. And then, they
turned their backs on Dumbo in a
solid wall. Now hidden in the hay
pile was Timothy Mouse, the circus
mouse. Timothy loved scaring
elephants, and he thought this
was the best time to do it.

"They can't treat the little fellow that way," he muttered, "not while Timothy Mouse is around." So he stepped out. "Boo! Boo!" he yelled. And the big brave elephants ran in all directions, leaving Timothy and Dumbo alone.

"**D**on't be afraid, little fellow," said Timothy Mouse to the baby elephant. "I'm your friend. I want to help you. What we have to do is find a use for those ears. You're the only one who has them. Those ears will make you famous. Then they'll let your mother out of prison, and we'll all live happily ever after. "Dumbo nodded happily. His ears flapped like sails.

"I've got it!" Timothy shouted. "You know the big elephant balancing act at the end of the show? Well, when they have their pyramid built, you'll jump on the acrobats' springboard and bounce right up to the top of that pyramid, waving a little flag. You'll be the star of the show. Let's sneak out and practice now!"

On their way to the practice field that Timothy had chosen, they passed the prison wagon where Mrs. Jumbo stood, sadly staring out into the night. How delighted she was to see her baby. And how happy Dumbo was to curl up safe in the curve of his mother's trunk once more. He told her all about the elephant act, how unhappy he was without her, and about the wonderful idea Timothy had for making him a success.

Finally, Timothy had to pull Dumbo away, so that they could practice springboard jumping before dawn, when they would have to be back with the elephants.

When Dumbo could jump from the springboard to a stand ten, fifteen, then twenty feet high, Timothy whispered his idea into the sleeping Ringmaster's ear.

And the very next day, as a surprise, Dumbo's jump was added as a highlight to the show.

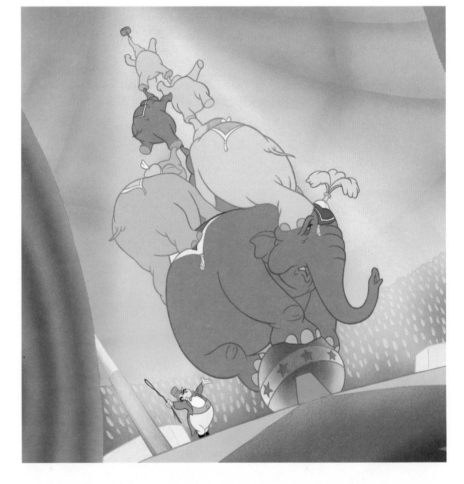

The great moment came. The pyramid of elephants was swaying in the ring. Dumbo ran down the springboard.

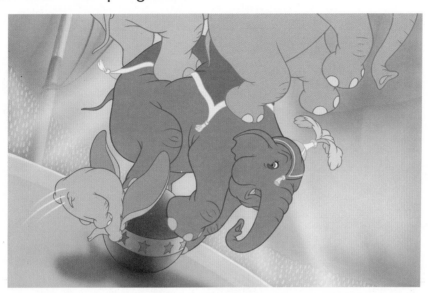

Then it happened. He tripped over his flapping ears! Up he bounced, in a twirling ball, and he crashed into that great pyramid of elephants, knocking them in every direction at once!

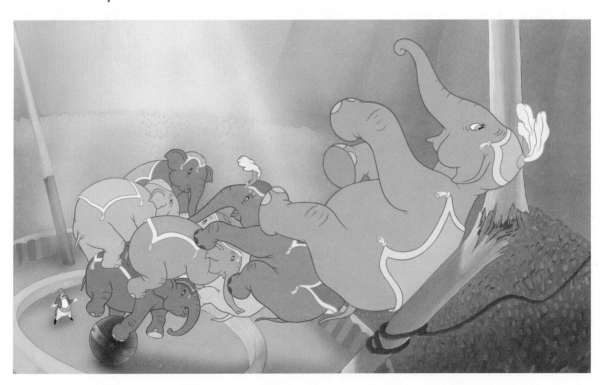

That was the finish! The next day, they made Dumbo into a clown. They painted his face with a foolish grin and dressed him in a baby dress. On his head they put a bonnet. And they used him in the most ridiculous act in the show—a make-believe fire.

Dumbo had to jump from the top of a blazing cardboard house, down into the clown-firemen's net. The audience thought it was a great joke. But Dumbo felt terrible. And he was frightened, too.

"Don't worry, Dumbo," Timothy whispered as he curled up in Dumbo's hat brim. "We'll have you starring in the show yet. You'll be flying high!" Back in the circus tent, curled up to sleep in the warm sweet hay, knowing that Timothy was close by, Dumbo fell asleep at once.

The next morning Timothy was the first to awaken. He stretched and sleepily looked around him. Close beside him, three black crows sat and stared at him. "What are you doing here?" Timothy asked sleepily. "What are **YOU** doing here?" snapped the crows.

At that, Timothy sat up and took another look around him. "Why—why, where am I?" he gasped. He was still in the brim of Dumbo's hat, and the hat was still on top of Dumbo's head. But Dumbo was asleep on the branch of a tree far, far above the ground!

"**H**ow did we get here?" Timothy asked. "Flew!" the crows cackled. "You and that elephant just came a-flyin' up." "Flying?" yelled Timothy. "Dumbo, Dumbo, you flew!" Slowly Dumbo opened his eyes. He glanced down. He gulped. Then he struggled to his feet. He tried to balance in the wobbly tree fork, but he slipped . . . down, down, down! He bounced from branch to branch, with Timothy clinging on for dear life.

PLONK! They landed in a brook beneath the tree. The crows chuckled and cawed from above.

Timothy scrambled up out of the water and wrung the brook water out of Dumbo's tail. "Dumbo!" he cried. "You can fly! If you can fly when you're asleep, you can fly when you're awake." So Dumbo tried again . . . and again . . . But he could not leave the ground. With Timothy as his teacher, Dumbo practiced for hours. He ran and he jumped and he hopped—and he tripped. He tried fast and slow takeoffs. He tried standing and running jumps. He counted as he flapped his ears—one-two-three-four. But as hard as he tried, Dumbo could not fly.

At last the crows felt sorry for him. "Here, try this magic feather," one of them said. "This is how we teach our babies to fly. Hold onto this and you'll be fine." Dumbo clutched the feather in the tip of his trunk, and he tried once more. The magic-feather trick worked like a charm.

No sooner had Dumbo wrapped his trunk around the feather than flap, flap, flap went his ears. Up into the air he soared like a bird. Over the tallest tree-tops he sailed. He glided, he dipped, and he dived. Three times he circled over the heads of the cheering crows.

Then he headed back to the circus grounds, with Timothy cheering as loud as he could cheer from the brim of Dumbo's clown hat. "We must keep your flying a secret—a surprise for this afternoon's show," Timothy decided. So they landed before they reached the tents. When they got back safely, without being missed, it was time for Dumbo to get into his costume for the big clown act. Then he had to wait inside the little cardboard house all through the show, until make-believe fire crackled up around him. But today he did not mind. Because Timothy was with him. **Cr-rr-rr-ack! Cr-rr-ack!** crackled the fire. **Clang! Clang!** roared the clown fire engine, rushing toward the blaze.

"Save my baby!" cried a clown, dressed up as a mother. That was Dumbo's cue to appear at the window. So Timothy tucked the magic feather into the curve of his trunk, and climbed to his place in Dumbo's hat brim. "Good luck, Dumbo!" he cried. The firemen brought a big net and held it out.

"Jump, my baby, jump!" shrieked the mother clown. Dumbo jumped, but as he jumped the magic feather slipped from his trunk and floated away. Now my magic is gone, Dumbo thought.

He plunged down like a stone. Timothy saw the feather drift past. He knew how Dumbo felt. "It's all right, Dumbo!" he shouted. "The feather was a trick! You can fly by yourself!" Dumbo heard the shout.

Doubtfully, he spread his ears wide. Just two feet above the firemen's net, he stopped his plunge and swooped up into the air! A mighty gasp arose from the audience. They knew it couldn't be . . . but it was! Dumbo was flying!

While the crowd roared with delight, Dumbo did power dives, loops, spins, and barrel rolls. He swooped down to pick up peanuts and squirted a trunkful of water on the clowns. The keepers freed Mrs. Jumbo and brought her to the tent in triumph to see her baby fly. Now all Dumbo's worries were over.

Soon Dumbo was a hero from coast to coast. Timothy became his manager and saw to it that Dumbo got a wonderful contract with a big salary and a pension for his mother. The circus was renamed Dumbo's Flying Circus, and Dumbo traveled in a special streamlined car.

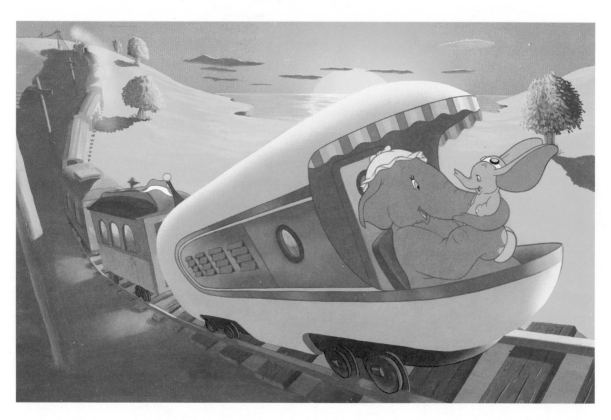

But best of all, he forgave everyone who had been unkind to him, for his heart was as big as his magical ears.

This is the story of Hercules, a great hero and the strongest man who ever walked the earth. But our story begins long before his birth....

Long ago, in ancient Greece, powerful gods ruled the Earth from their sanctuary on Mount Olympus.

The greatest of the gods by far was the mighty Zeus. Zeus organized the rest of the gods to conquer the evil Titans, gigantic troublemakers who had caused great chaos—tormenting the people with catastrophic earthquakes, tidal waves, and volcanic blasts.

But now, the Titans were safely locked away where they could do no more harm. Under the wise guidance of Zeus, the earth was a peaceful and orderly place, and the people were happy. So were the gods.

So of course there was great celebration when a son was born to Zeus and his beautiful wife, the goddess Hera. The baby Hercules was bathed in a heavenly glow, and wore a gold medallion.

When news of Hercules' birth spread, all of the gods and goddesses gathered at Zeus's palace to admire the new baby, and to shower him with a mountain of fabulous gifts.

Zeus was very proud of his son.

Especially when the baby grabbed hold of his father's finger, and lifted him right off the ground!

"This child is strong, just like his dad!" laughed Zeus.

Then Hera nudged her husband, "Where's our gift, dear?"

Zeus formed a puff of clouds with his hands and spun the clouds into the shape of a baby horse. Out stepped a colt with white wings.

"His name is Pegasus, Son," said Zeus. "And he's all yours." Baby Hercules cooed and gurgled and stretched out his arms.

Meanwhile, Hades, god of the Underworld, had arrived at the party and was watching with a fierce scowl. Hades was not exactly crazy about Zeus and his happy little family. Thanks to Zeus, Hades was in charge of the gloomy Underworld. While the other gods whooped it up on Mount Olympus, he had to spend his time surrounded by a bunch of lost souls and dead-heads. On top of that, he had to put up with a giant three-headed guard dog that kept attacking him, as well as some very annoying demons

So by the time Hades got home to the Underworld, he had figured out what he wanted…revenge!

Two demons, Pain and Panic, were waiting for him on the dock. "Let me know the instant the Fates arrive," Hades growled.

The Fates were three ugly crones who shared only one eye between them but could see the future. "So let me just ask…is this Hercules—is this kid gonna mess up my hostile takeover bid or what?" Hades demanded.

The Fates were not supposed to reveal the future to anyone, but Hades wormed the truth out of them.

They told him that in 18 years, when the planets lined up, he would have his only chance to take over the world. But, they warned, "should Hercules fight, you will fail."

"WHAT?" Hades exploded. When he calmed down, he remembered the rules. No one could kill a god—gods were immortal. He would have to make Hercules mortal.

So he gave the demons Pain and Panic a magic potion and sent them off to kidnap the baby Hercules.

Hercules found the ride through the night air quite a lot of fun. But when the demons landed on Earth, Hercules yelled.

Hercules' cry wakened a farmer and his wife, and they dashed outdoors to see what was going on. "Who's there?" the farmer called into the darkness.

Pain and Panic dropped Hercules before he had finished the potion and hid themselves behind some bushes.

"Why you poor thing," the wife said when she saw the baby. Because of the potion, Hercules had already lost his god-like glow. He looked like a normal baby—and the couple had been praying for a child for a long time.

"Amphitryon, for so many years we prayed to the gods to bless us with a child. Perhaps they've answered our prayers," the farmer said. Then he noticed the gold medallion the baby wore. "Hercules," he read.

Pain and Panic knew they had to finish their job. But when they changed into snakes and slithered out from the bushes to attack the farmer and his wife, baby Hercules snatched them up by their snaky tails, tied them together in a knot, and hurled them screaming far into the distance. The farmer and his wife stared at him in amazement.

Panic said. "Hades is gonna kill us when he finds out what happened!"

"You mean *if* he finds out," said Pain.

Meanwhile, Hercules had become almost mortal. But because he had not finished the potion, he kept his god-like strength.

He grew up thinking that Amphitryon and his wife were his parents. But his enormous strength sometimes created problems. When he tried to join a group of boys playing a game of discus in the village, he accidentally bumped into some stone pillars, and destroyed the marketplace.

"**D**estructo-boy," the townspeople called him. "What a geek!" they shouted. "Freak!" They wanted Hercules' father to keep him away from them. "That boy is a menace!" someone said.

Back home, the farmer said, "Son, you shouldn't let those things they said back there get to you."

"But, Pop, they're right. I am a freak!" Hercules hung his head. "Sometimes I feel like...like I really don't belong here. Like I'm supposed to be someplace else."

The farmer and his wife knew it was time to tell Hercules the truth. They told him how they had found him as a baby, and they showed him the gold medallion. "This was around your neck when we found you. It's the symbol of the gods."

Hercules realized that he had to find out where he came from—to find a place where he fit in. "Maybe the gods have the answers," he said. He put the medallion around his neck, and said goodbye to the only parents he knew. "You're the greatest parents anyone could have, but I gotta know...."

So Hercules traveled to the temple of Zeus. He prayed before a huge statue. "Oh, mighty Zeus, please hear me and answer my prayer. I need to know. Who am I? Where do I belong?"

With a flash of lightning the statue came alive. Hercules was terrified, and tried to run away, but Zeus picked the boy up.

"Is this the kind of 'hello' you give your father?" Zeus said.

Hercules was astonished. "F-f-father?" he stammered. "If you're my father, that would make me a..."

"A god," Zeus said. And he told Hercules the whole story, about how he was kidnapped and became mortal. The problem was, he explained, that Hercules could not return to Mount Olympus because he was no longer immortal.

"You can't do a thing?" Hercules asked.

"I can't, Hercules. But you can," Zeus replied. "If you can prove yourself a true hero on Earth, your godhood will be restored."

"Great!" Hercules said. "Uh…exactly how do you become a true hero?"

The first step, Zeus explained, was to find Philoctetes, the trainer of heroes.

Hercules was so eager to begin that he ran for the door. "Whoa! Hold your horses!" Zeus said. "Which reminds me…"

Zeus whistled, and a great white winged horse flew in from the sky. "You probably don't remember Pegasus," Zeus said.

But as soon as the horse nuzzled Hercules, he found he did remember. He mounted Pegasus, and together they flew into the sky.

Philoctetes was a tubby little fellow with the horns and hind legs of a goat. "Call me Phil," the satyr said.

"I need your help," Hercules said. "I want to become a hero. A true hero."

"Sorry, kid. I can't help ya," Phil said. "Two words: I am retired."

Phil was tired of training heroes; they all ended up disappointing him. But he changed his mind when Zeus hit him with a lightning bolt. So the next day, Hercules began learning all of the skills a hero needs. And he and Phil became good friends.

After months of training, it was time for Hercules to test his skills in real life. "We're going to Thebes," Phil said. "It's a big, tough town. Good place to start building a rep."

But on the way, Hercules and Pegasus heard the cry of a damsel in distress. Hercules rushed to help her. The young woman was struggling to free herself from the clutches of a huge, shaggy centaur—half man and half horse.

Strangely, the woman didn't seem to want help. "Back off!" she said. "I can handle this." But after a struggle, Hercules walloped the centaur.

"Are you all right, Miss, uh…?" Hercules asked shyly.

"Megara. My friends call me Meg," she said, batting her eyelashes.

Megara refused Hercules' offer of a ride, and he watched her walk away. "She's something. Isn't she, Phil?" he said.

"Yeah," answered Phil. "A real pain in the patella!" Then Phil reminded Hercules that they were supposed to be in Thebes.

As Hercules, Phil, and Pegasus continued on their way to Thebes, Megara headed deep into the woods until Hades appeared. "What exactly happened here?" he asked. "I thought you were going to persuade the River Guardian to join my team for the uprising...."

"Look, it wasn't my fault," Meg pleaded. "It was this Wonder Boy, Hercules."

"Hercules?!" Hades shouted, grabbing Pain and Panic by their tails. "So you took care of him, eh?

"Fortunately for the three of you," Hades growled, "we still have time to correct this." Hades had already come up with another plan to get rid of Hercules.

When Hercules and Phil finally got to Thebes, the streets were filled with people, all complaining about the state of their city. Crime was on the rise, and there were floods, fires, and earthquakes.

Of course, Hercules offered to help. "I'm Hercules, and, uh…I happen to be a hero," he said.

But no one took him seriously. In fact, they laughed, which angered Phil. He tried to convince them that Hercules was the real thing, but the crowd laughed ever harder. Finally, Phil butted one man with his horns. Hercules had to break up the fight.

Just then, Hercules heard a voice calling, "Help, please! There's been a terrible accident!"

It was Meg. She explained that two little boys had been trapped by a rock slide.

They climbed onto Pegasus and flew to where the boys were pinned beneath a gigantic boulder. Hercules lifted it easily, and the children scampered away.

Little did Hercules know that Meg had led him into a trap. The boys were really Pain and Panic in disguise. The next moment, Hercules was attacked by a dragon-like monster. The Hydra had been lying in wait behind the boulder.

The Hydra swallowed Hercules in one gulp, but he slashed his way out with his sword, and then sliced off the creature's giant head.

By this time a crowd had gathered, and they cheered wildly. But then Hercules heard a hissing sound from the monster's neck. Out popped three heads where one had been!

Every time Hercules sliced off a head, three more grew to replace it. Finally the monster had thirty heads—all chomping and hissing!

This wasn't working. Hercules stopped to think. Then he smashed his fist into the mountainside and caused a landslide that buried the Hydra and Hercules both.

Phil was devastated. The crowd was silent…and then Hercules emerged from the rubble, and the crowd went wild.

From that day on, people cheered when Hercules rode past. The merchants of Thebes sold souvenirs depicting his victory. Hercules continued his heroics, battling monsters and overcoming disasters wherever he found them, his faithful friend Phil at his side.

After a string of successes, Hercules felt certain he had proven himself. So he and Pegasus traveled to Mount Olympus to see his father.

Zeus looked pleased with what Hercules reported. "You're doing great, son," he said.

"I've been waiting for this day a long time," Hercules said.

"Hmmm, what day is that, son?" asked Zeus.

"The day I rejoin the gods."

A shadow crossed Zeus's face, "My boy, I'm afraid being famous isn't the same as being a true hero."

"What more can I do?"

"Look inside your heart," said Zeus.

Hercules was frustrated. He lost interest in the job of being a hero. So when Meg showed up and suggested that he play hooky from the hero business for a day, Hercules was happy to agree. He never suspected that Hades was behind her visit....

Hades was running out of time. The day the Fates had predicted was approaching—the day the planets would be in perfect alignment and Hades could take over the world.

Only Hercules stood in his way. And Hades still had not discovered the hero's fatal weakness. In fact, so far, Hercules had evaded every trap Hades had set for him.

Meg had had enough of helping Hades. "I've done my part," she said.

That's when Hades reminded her that she had sold him her soul. He offered Meg her freedom in return for her cooperation.

So Meg had set out to discover Hercules' fatal weakness. But her heart wasn't in it.

Hercules and Meg spent a glorious day together, wandering through his gardens and chatting. By evening, Hercules knew he was falling in love with her, and confessed his deepest hopes and fears.

"When I'm with you, I don't feel so…alone," he admitted.

Meg's problem was that she was also falling in love with Hercules. She didn't want to hurt him, but Hades had her in his power. What could she do?

"Get yourself another girl," Meg told Hades.

But Hades wouldn't allow Meg to stop working for him. And Phil happened to hear enough of the conversation to figure out that Meg had been working for Hades. He raced to warn Hercules.

"She's a fraud!" Phil cried "She's nothing but a two-timing, no-good, lying—"

"Shut up!" Hercules shouted.

Phil stormed off. "That's it."

So Hercules was alone when Hades showed up with Meg, tightly bound in chains of cloud. "Give up your strength for about twenty-four hours," Hades said, "and Meg here is free as a bird and safe from harm."

Hercules couldn't bear to see Meg suffer. He agreed to the deal, and the next thing he knew, Hades had drained the power from his body.

As he released Meg, Hades told Hercules that she had been working for him all along.

Hades had only twenty-four hours left, and lots to do. First, he released the Titans from the pit where Zeus had imprisoned them. "Look at your squalid prison. Who put you down there?"

"Zeus!" the Titans roared.

"And if I release you, what's the first thing you're gonna do?"

"Destroy him!"

Next, Hades went to find the giant one-eyed Cyclops. "I have a special job for you," he said.

So the Titans attacked Mount Olympus. The gods barely had time to prepare themselves for battle. Zeus knew Hades was behind the attack, but he was powerless against the Titans.

The Cyclops was on the rampage in Thebes and the terrified citizens called for help as they tried to get away from the monster.

Hercules headed for the commotion. "Stop!" Meg shouted. "Without your strength, you'll be killed!" But Hercules, convinced that Meg had betrayed him, didn't care whether he lived or died.

Meg went to find Phil. Maybe he could talk some sense into Hercules.

By the time Meg returned with Phil, Hercules was battered and dazed, and had nearly given up. But Phil urged him on. "Come on, kid! Fight back," he shouted. "Giving up is for rookies."

So with his last shred of strength, Hercules wrapped a rope around the giant's ankles and toppled him into the sea.

As the Cyclops fell, he knocked over two huge columns. "Hercules! Look out!" Meg cried, pushing Hercules out of the way. One column fell on Meg, pinning her underneath it.

As Hercules strained to move it, he felt his strength returning. It was because Hades had broken his deal—he had promised Meg would be safe, but now she was badly injured. Hercules held her in his arms. "Meg, why did you…? You didn't have to—"

"People always do crazy things when they're in love," Meg whispered. Hercules was speechless. "You can still stop Hades," Meg added.

So Hercules and Pegasus sped to Mount Olympus, leaving Phil to look after Meg. They arrived to find the gods already in chains, tormented by the Titans.

Hercules broke the gods' bonds, saying, "This ought to even up the odds."

Then he smashed through the frozen lava that imprisoned Zeus. "Thank you, my boy," Zeus said. "Now watch your old man work." Grabbing a load of thunderbolts, he hurled them at the Titans.

The Titans shrieked and tried to scatter, but Hercules hurled them into space.

An angry Hades watched from his chariot. "At least I got one swell consolation prize," he called to Hercules. "A friend of yours who's dying to see me."

Meg! Hercules jumped onto Pegasus, praying he wouldn't be too late.

But when he landed backed in Thebes, Phil's tearful face told the whole story. Meg was dead. "I'm sorry kid, but there's some things ya just can't change."

"Yes, I can," Hercules vowed.

Back in the Underworld, Hades was still fuming about his defeat when the gates of the throne room burst open, and in came Hercules, riding on the three-headed watchdog, Cerberus.

"Where's Meg?" Hercules demanded. Through an archway, he caught sight of a swirling mass of souls, Meg among them. He reached out his hand, but pulled back in horror. His hand had begun to age.

"You like making deals," Hercules said. "Take me in Meg's place."

Hades considered. "Okay. You get her out, she goes, you stay."

Hercules dived into the Pit of Death. As he swam after Meg, his body aged until he was hardly more than a skeleton. Then, to Hades' amazement, Hercules' body turned back to normal, and began to glow. He emerged from the pit carrying Meg's soul.

"You can't be alive!" Hades said, "You'd have to be…"

"A god?" chimed Pain and Panic.

Hades tried to make another deal, but Hercules just grabbed him and threw him into the Pit of Death.

Hercules guided Meg's spirit back to her lifeless body. As Phil and Pegasus looked on, her eyelids fluttered, then opened. Hercules helped her to her feet.

As they held each other, lightning bolts struck the ground around them, and a cloud billowed beneath their feet. The cloud rose slowly upward, and carried them to the gates of Mount Olympus.

As Hercules started up the stairs, all the gods gave him a standing ovation.

The goddess Hera, his mother, greeted him. "Hercules, we're so proud of you."

Hera hugged him. "You were willing to give your life to rescue this young woman…" she said.

"…for a true hero isn't measured by the size of his strength but by the strength of his heart," Zeus said. "Now, at last, my son, you can come home."

Meg looked up at Hercules, tears in her eyes. "Congratulations, Wonder Boy. You'll make one heck of a god."

Hercules had always dreamed of this moment, but it took him only a heartbeat to make his decision.

He turned to his father. "A life without Meg, even an immortal one, would be…empty," he said. He took Meg's hands, and she brightened through her tears. "I wish to stay on Earth with her. I finally know where I belong."

Zeus and Hera were disappointed at losing their son, but they respected his wishes.

In the heavens, Zeus formed a new constellation of stars in the sky, to honor his heroic son.

And Hercules at last knew what his father had meant: heroic deeds are born in the heart.

It was a very important day in the Pride Lands. All the animals that lived there came from far and wide to celebrate the birth of King Mufasa's son. Rafiki, the wise old mystic, made a special mark on the new prince Simba's head. Mufasa and Queen Sarabi, Simba's mother, looked on with pride.

Then Rafiki held the cub high, at the edge of Pride Rock, so that all the animals gathered below could see their future king. The animals cheered for Simba, as he looked around bewildered. Then they all fell silent, and bowed to show their respect for him.

Mufasa's brother, Scar, was the only one missing from the ceremony. King Mufasa went to speak to his brother.

"Sarabi and I didn't see you at the presentation of Simba," said Mufasa when he reached Scar's cave.

"That was today?" Scar said in mock innocence. "Must have slipped my mind."

"Yes, well, as slippery as your mind is, as the king's brother, you should have been first in line," said Zazu, Mufasa's majordomo.

"I was first in line until that little hairball was born," replied Scar.

"That hairball is my son, and your future king," said Mufasa angrily.

Mufasa knew that Scar was smoldering with jealousy and anger because the young prince Simba had taken his place as next in line to be king. "What am I going to do with him?" worried Mufasa.

When Simba was a little older, Mufasa led him to the top of Pride Rock one morning at dawn.

"Everything the light touches is our kingdom," he explained. "One day, Simba, the sun will set on my time here and will rise with you as the new king!"

"What about that shadowy place?" asked Simba, looking into the distance.

"That's beyond our borders. You must never go there, Simba," Mufasa replied soberly.

"But I thought a king can do whatever he wants," Simba said.

"There's more to being king than getting your way all the time," his father replied.

Mufasa tried to explain to Simba what being king was all about. "Everything you see exists together in a delicate balance. As king, you need to understand that balance and respect all the creatures," Mufasa said. "We are all connected in the great circle of life."

But then news of invading hyenas arrived, and Mufasa had to leave Simba alone.

Later that day, Scar told Simba what that shadowy place was. "Only the bravest lions go there," he said slyly. "An elephant graveyard is no place for a young prince."

"Whoa!" Simba said.

Of course, the young lion couldn't resist proving how brave he was, so he ran to get his best friend, Nala.

"Come on!" said Simba. "I just heard about this great place!"

The two cubs soon escaped the watchful eyes of Zazu, who was supposed to baby-sit them. They headed for the shadowy place. Suddenly, they came upon an enormous, hollow-eyed skull. "This is it!" Simba announced.

"Whoa!" Nala said. "It's really creepy!"

"I know," Simba replied. "Let's go check it out!" He was about to climb into one of the huge eye sockets when Zazu caught up to them.

"We're way beyond the boundary of the Pride Lands," he said. "We are all in very real danger."

"I laugh in the face of danger!" exclaimed Simba. "Ha, ha!"

"Ha, ha!" answered the elephant skull. Suddenly, three hyenas appeared. They were not pleased that Simba and his friends had trespassed into their territory. They laughed their evil laugh before circling the threesome.

Zazu suggested that it was a good time to leave.

"What's the hurry?" Shenzi, one of the hyenas, said. "We'd love you to stick around for dinner."

"Yeah," Banzai added. "We could have whatever's 'lion' around, get it?"

The hyenas rolled on the ground with laughter—they loved a good pun. They kept coming up with new ones until they realized that their dinner was silently tiptoeing away.

The hyenas caught Zazu by the tail while the trio was making its escape. Simba returned to try to rescue the bird. He growled his most vicious growl at the hyenas.

"Why don't you pick on somebody your own size?" he shouted.

When Shenzi went after Nala, Simba scratched the hyena on the nose. The hyenas chased Simba and Nala into the rib cage of an old carcass, which snapped closed, trapping them inside like the bars of a jail.

As the hyenas crept towards the trapped lion cubs, they chuckled softly. Their long, sharp teeth gleamed in the dim light. Just when Simba and Nala were sure all hope was lost, a huge paw slammed at Shenzi, knocking her down and sending the other hyenas flying.

It was Mufasa, and he had arrived just in time. The hyenas were no match for him.

"If you ever come near my son again…" the Lion King roared.

The beaten hyenas fled with their tails between their legs.

"Zazu," Mufasa ordered, "take Nala home. I've got to teach my son a lesson."

When they were alone, he continued, "Simba, I'm very disappointed in you."

Simba tried to explain his behavior. "I was just trying to be brave like you."

"Simba, being brave doesn't mean you go looking for trouble," Mufasa said.

"But you're not scared of anything!" Simba insisted.

"I was today," his father said. "I thought I might lose you."

The Lion King and his prince looked up at the stars. "The great kings of the past look down on us from those stars," Mufasa said. "Those kings will always be there to guide you…and so will I."

Mufasa didn't realize that his own brother Scar was plotting to harm him and his son, in order to take the throne.

The next day, Scar led Simba into a steep gorge, telling him that Mufasa had a surprise for him. He left his nephew there, then signaled to the hyenas, who started a stampede of wildebeests through the gorge.

As Simba hung onto a tree for dear life, Scar yelled to Mufasa, "Quick! Stampede! In the gorge! Simba's down there!"

Mufasa leapt into the gorge and snatched the cub out of the path of the deadly hooves. He set Simba safely on a rocky ledge. But then the rock crumbled under Mufasa's paws, and he fell into the herd of wildebeests.

Mufasa was badly injured. Gathering all his strength, he tried to crawl back out of the gorge. Near the top, he saw Scar waiting for him on the ledge. "Brother, help me!" Mufasa begged.

Scar leaned down toward Mufasa. He pulled his brother close and whispered, "Long live the king!" Then Scar let go of Mufasa, and he fell into the stampeding herd.

The cub raced into the gorge, calling for his father. But when Simba finally reached Mufasa, the great Lion King was dead.

While Simba grieved, Scar suddenly appeared out of the dust. "Simba," he said, "what have you done?"

"He tried to save me," Simba answered. "It was an accident. I didn't mean for it to…"

"The king is dead," Scar said. "If it weren't for you, he'd still be alive!"

"What am I gonna do?" Simba sobbed.

"Run away, Simba…run away and never return!" Scar told him.

Confused and heartbroken, Simba began to run. But he soon realized that the hyenas were following him. They chased the cub all the way to the edge of a plateau. There was only one way out. Simba leapt off the cliff into a tangle of thorns.

The hyenas were afraid of getting hurt in the thorns. Instead of following Simba, they shouted, "If you ever come back, we'll kill ya!"

With Mufasa and Simba gone, Scar was now the ruler of the Pride Lands. On his way to the top of Pride Rock to announce himself king, Scar made an announcement to the lions gathered below. "Mufasa's death is a terrible tragedy. But to lose Simba, who had barely begun to live… For me, it is a deep, personal loss."

Sarabi, Nala, and the other lionesses began to mourn.

"It is with a heavy heart," Scar continued, "that I assume the throne."

The wise Rafiki watched from a distance, shaking his head in disbelief.

Meanwhile, injured and exhausted, Simba stumbled across the hot African desert. Vultures circled above him. Finally, unable to go any further, he fainted. When he awoke, a meerkat and a warthog were standing over him. They had pulled him to an oasis and splashed water on him.

"You okay, kid?" asked the meerkat.

"You nearly died," said the warthog.

"Where ya from?" the meerkat asked.

"Who cares?" Simba said quietly. "I can't go back."

"Ah, you're an outcast!" cried the meerkat. "So are we!" Timon, the meerkat, and Pumbaa, the warthog, tried to encourage their new friend. "You gotta put your past behind you," they told Simba. *"Hakuna matata!"*

Simba followed Timon and Pumbaa to their jungle home. He soon adapted to their diet of bugs and grubs—as well as their easygoing lifestyle.

Time passed, and Simba grew into a young lion. He was happy, except when he thought about his father.

One day, he heard his friends cry out for help. He found Pumbaa stuck under a tree root, while a hungry lioness approached him. Simba quickly leapt into action and pounced on her. As the lions tussled, Timon gave Pumbaa a blow-by-blow account. "Get her! Bite her head! Go for the jugular!" Timon cried.

The lioness had Simba pinned to the ground when she suddenly paused. She and Simba looked into each other's eyes.

"Nala?" Simba asked incredulously. "It's me! Simba!"

Nala was delighted to find her childhood friend.

Simba introduced everyone, but Nala could not stop staring at him. "Everyone thinks you're dead," she said.

"They do?" Simba asked.

"Yes," she replied. "Scar told us about the stampede."

"What else did he tell you?" Simba asked warily.

"What else matters?" Nala cried. "You're alive! And that means you're the king!"

"King?" Timon and Pumbaa looked at each other in shock.

Simba and Nala went off into the forest to talk. Nala told Simba all about Scar. "Simba, he let the hyenas take over the Pride Lands," Nala said. "Everything's destroyed. There's no food, no water. If you don't do something soon, everyone will starve."

Simba hung his head and replied, "I can't go back."

Nala could not understand why Simba would not help the pride. "What's happened to you?" she asked. "You're not the Simba I remember."

"Listen!" he said angrily. "You think you can just show up and tell me how to live my life? You don't even know what I've been through."

That night, Simba was still thinking about his decision when an old baboon appeared. It was wise Rafiki! He told Simba that he could help him understand who he was and what he should do.

"I know your father," Rafiki said.

"I hate to tell you this, but he died a long time ago," Simba replied.

"Nope! Wrong again! He's alive," the baboon said. "I'll show him to you." He led Simba to a pool of water and pointed to Simba's reflection.

A breeze rippled the water, and Simba saw his father's face.

"You see?" Rafiki asked. "He lives in you!"

Then Simba heard a familiar voice calling his name. He looked up at the stars and saw Mufasa's image.

"You are more than what you have become," Mufasa said, "You must take your place in the Circle of Life."

"How can I go back?" Simba replied. "I'm not who I used to be."

"Remember who you are....You are my son and the one true king...." Mufasa's answer echoed in the still night. "Remember...."

Then his father's image disappeared, and Simba was all alone.

Simba finally made up his mind to return home. As he crossed into his kingdom, he saw devastation everywhere. The great herds were gone. The grasslands were dead.

Nala, Timon, and Pumbaa soon caught up to Simba. When they saw some hyenas, Timon and Pumbaa distracted them while Simba and Nala headed for Pride Rock.

Meanwhile, at Pride Rock, the hyenas complained to Scar that the lionesses had not brought them any food for days.

"Scar, there is no food. The herds have moved on," Sarabi explained. Their only hope was to leave Pride Rock.

"We're not going anywhere," Scar growled.

"Then you have sentenced us to death," Sarabi replied.

"So be it," Scar said. "I am the king. I can do whatever I want!"

"If you were half the king Mufasa was…" Sarabi began. But the mere mention of Mufasa's name enraged Scar.

As Scar roared at Sarabi, he looked up and saw a great lion outlined against a blaze of lightning.

At first Scar thought that he was seeing Mufasa's ghost, but Sarabi recognized her son. "Simba!" she cried.

"Step down, Scar!" Simba said.

But Scar wasn't ready to give up. "If it weren't for you, Mufasa would still be alive! It's your fault he's dead!" Scar said slyly.

"Tell me it's not true!" cried Sarabi.

Scar and the hyenas quickly surrounded Simba. They forced him right off the edge of a cliff. Simba held on for dear life.

Scar looked down at Simba. "Now, this looks familiar," he sneered. "Where have I seen this before? Oh yes…This is just the way your father looked before he died….I killed Mufasa."

Now that Simba finally knew the truth about his father's death, his anger gave him strength, and he leapt toward his uncle.

Scar roared at the hyenas for help.

But Simba had friends, too. Nala and the other lionesses, as well as Timon and Pumbaa, attacked the hyenas. Scar took advantage of the confusion to sneak away.

He didn't get far, though, because Simba spotted his uncle at the edge of Pride Rock, and cornered him.

Scar begged for mercy. "It's the hyenas who are the real enemy," he said. "It was their fault—it was their idea!" Little did Scar know that the hyenas overheard his betrayal.

But Simba didn't believe his uncle. He repeated the advice Scar had given him years before. "Run away, Scar, and never return," he commanded.

Scar lunged at Simba. When Simba moved out of the way, Scar fell over the edge of the cliff. Simba could hear the sounds of hungry hyenas drifting up from the gorge, revealing his uncle's awful fate.

As rain began to fall, Simba stood at the edge of Pride Rock and roared triumphantly. The lionesses roared back with joy. The rest of the hyenas fled and were never seen again.

Soon, under the wise and brave Simba, the Pride Lands flourished. The herd returned to graze, the grasslands grew back, and food was plentiful again.

Not long afterwards, the animals gathered once more to celebrate the birth of the king's cub.

Simba and Nala watched proudly as Rafiki held their new cub high over Pride Rock.

Simba remembered his father telling him, "A king's time as ruler rises and falls like the sun. One day the sun will set on my time here and rise with you as the new ruler."

Simba would someday pass these same words on to his own cub, and the Circle of Life would continue.

Once upon a time in a faraway land, a young Prince lived in a shining castle. Although he had everything his heart desired, he was selfish and unkind.

One winter's night, an Enchantress came to the castle disguised as an old beggar woman. She offered him a single rose in return for shelter from the cold. But the Prince sneered at her gift, and turned her away.

So the Enchantress transformed him into a hideous beast, and transformed all his servants into household objects. The spell would be broken only if the Beast could learn to love, and earn someone's love in return before the last petal fell from the enchanted rose.

Ashamed of his ugliness, the Beast locked himself away in his castle. An enchanted mirror was his only window to the outside world.

As the years passed, he lost all hope. For who could ever love a beast?

Not far from the castle, in a small village, lived a beautiful girl named Belle. Belle loved to read tales of far-off places, magic spells, and princes in disguise. She yearned for excitement in her life, and for someone with whom to share it.

That someone was definitely not the handsome Gaston, who had announced his intention to marry Belle because she was the most beautiful girl in the village. Belle considered Gaston self-centered and arrogant. Besides, she had other plans.

Belle's father, Maurice, was an inventor, although most of his inventions failed. "I'm about ready to give up on this hunk of junk," Maurice said one day, kicking his latest project.

"You always say that," Belle laughed. "But I just know you'll win first prize at the fair."

With Belle's encouragement, Maurice finally finished one of his inventions. That afternoon, he packed it onto the wagon behind his horse, Phillipe, and headed for the fair.

Hours later, they were still on the road. "We'll have to take a short cut through the woods," Maurice decided.

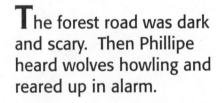

The forest road was dark and scary. Then Phillipe heard wolves howling and reared up in alarm.

"Whoa, Phillipe, whoa!" Maurice cried. But the terrified horse bolted and threw his rider.

Maurice had to flee from the wolves on foot. Just when he felt his strength would give out, he stumbled through the rusty gates of a gloomy castle.

No one answered his knock, so Maurice stepped cautiously inside the door. "Hello?" he called.

"Shh! Not a word," a mantel clock whispered to a golden candelabrum.

"Oh, Cogsworth, have a heart," the candelabrum replied. Then he called out, "You are welcome here, monsieur."

Maurice was astonished to see a talking candelabrum. But when Lumiere invited him to warm himself by the fire, he sank gratefully into a giant chair.

By the time Mrs. Potts arrived with her son, Chip, to offer Maurice a nice cup of tea, he was quite enjoying himself. "What service!" he said.

Just then, however, the door burst open, and the Beast's shadow fell over the room. 'What are you doing here?" he growled.

The next thing Maurice knew, great claws had grabbed him and hauled him off to a barred cell in the dungeon.

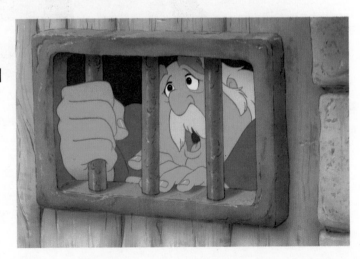

Back in the village, Belle was waiting for her father to return when Gaston swaggered in with a proposal.

"Picture this," he said. "A hunting lodge, my latest kill roasting on the fire, and my little wife massaging my feet. And do you know who that little wife will be? You Belle!"

Belle couldn't think what to say. Finally, she replied, "I'm very sorry, Gaston, but I just don't deserve you." As she maneuvered to get away from him, Gaston fell out the doorway and into a mud puddle, right in front of all the villagers. "I'll have Belle as my wife," he fumed. "Make no mistake about that."

But Belle didn't hear him, for at that moment, Phillipe galloped into the yard.

"Where's Papa?" Belle cried. "You have to take me to him!"

The tired horse carried Belle back through the woods. When she saw her father's hat on the ground inside the gate, she knew she had to enter the forbidding castle.

Lumiere took one look at Belle, and realized she was the one they had all been waiting for, the one who would break the spell. So he led the girl to her father.

"Oh, Papa! We have to get you out of here!" Belle cried. But just then, the Beast entered.

"**P**lease let my father out. He's sick," Belle begged.

"He shouldn't have trespassed," the Beast replied, "There's nothing you can do. He's my prisoner."

"Take me, instead," Belle said.

"Then you must promise to stay here forever," the Beast replied.

So it was agreed. The Beast dragged Maurice out the door to an enchanted carriage and sent him home.

Belle was heartbroken as she watched her father leave. She had not even been allowed to say good-bye. But she knew she had to keep her promise to the Beast.

Then the Wardrobe in her bedroom told her that the Beast wasn't as bad as he appeared. And the food at the castle was delicious. So Belle tried to make the best of things.

Meanwhile, as soon as he returned to the village, Maurice burst into the tavern shouting, "Help! He's got Belle locked in a dungeon!" But when he spoke of "a horrible beast," the villagers decided the old inventor was crazy.

While the others laughed at Maurice, Gaston took his friend Lefou aside. "I have a plan," he said. He had thought of a way to try to convince Belle to marry him.

At the castle, Belle was not locked up at all. The Beast had given her permission to go anywhere in the castle she wanted...except the West Wing.

Soon, the West Wing was all Belle could think about. So when no one was looking, she crept in. She found a dirty room full of cracked mirrors and broken furniture. The only beautiful, living thing was the enchanted rose, glowing inside a bell jar.

She was about to touch it when the Beast roared at her. "Why did you come here?" he bellowed. "Get out!"

Belle was terrified. Lumiere and Cogsworth saw her as she ran through the halls, but they could not stop her.

She ran out the front door, saddled Phillipe and escaped into the freezing night.

As Belle and Phillipe raced through the woods, they glimpsed the wild yellow eyes of wolves in the darkness. But when they tried to run faster, Phillipe's reins caught on a tree branch. He reared up in fear, and Belle was thrown to the ground. Instantly, snarling wolves surrounded her.

Suddenly, the Beast's giant paw snatched one of the wolves and tossed him through the air. After a fierce battle, the wolves fled, whining into the forest. But the Beast had been hurt.

Belle was about to jump back on the horse when she noticed that the Beast had collapsed in pain. She hesitated only a moment before running to his side.

Belle helped the Beast back to the enchanted castle, and nursed his wounds until he was better. Before long, Belle and the Beast were reading books, eating meals, and taking walks together.

"Isn't it wonderful!" the enchanted objects agreed as they watched the couple becoming friends.

Finally, the Beast allowed the enchanted objects to dress him in new clothes.

"Tonight, when the moment is right, you must confess your love to her," Lumiere advised the Beast.

So that night, after dinner, the Beast led Belle into the ballroom and they danced together to a beautiful love song.

"Belle, are you happy here with me?" the Beast asked.

"Yes, but..." Belle said, "if only I could see my father, just for a moment."

"There is a way," the Beast told her. And then he brought out his enchanted mirror.

When Belle looked into the mirror, she saw her father lost and shivering in the woods, searching for her. "He's sick! He may be dying!" she said.

"Then you must go to him," the Beast said. "I release you. But take the mirror with you, so you will always have a way to look back...and remember me."

"How can you let her go?" Cogsworth asked, near tears.

"Because I love her," the Beast replied.

With the mirror's help, Belle found her father and took him home. "How did you escape from that horrible beast?" her father asked.

"I didn't escape, Papa. He let me go," Belle said. "He's changed somehow."

Meanwhile, Gaston had convinced the director of the insane asylum to lock up Maurice. His plan was simple. He would convince Belle that he was the only one who could save her father, but only if she agreed to marry him.

"**E**veryone knows her father is a lunatic, talking about some giant beast. But Belle will do anything to protect him," Gaston explained.

But when Gaston and the director arrived, followed by a crowd of curious villagers, Belle held up the enchanted mirror, and showed them the image of the Beast. "My father's not crazy!" she protested. "The Beast is real, but he's also kind."

Gaston realized that Belle had feelings for the Beast. Enraged, he snatched the mirror from her.

"She's as crazy as her old man!" he told the crowd. "The Beast will make off with your children. I say we kill him!"

And so the angry crowd followed Gaston through the woods to storm the Beast's castle.

The enchanted household objects saw the mob from the castle windows, and prepared their defense. By the time the villagers battered through the castle door, an army of angry objects was ready for them.

"Now!" Lumiere yelled, leading the attack. Immediately, forks and brooms and furniture and objects of every description hurled themselves through the air towards the astonished townspeople.

But the Beast, sure he had lost Belle forever, had no heart for fighting. "What shall we do, master?" Mrs. Potts asked him.

"It doesn't matter now. Let them come," the Beast replied. So when Gaston stormed into his room, the Beast didn't even attempt to defend himself.

When Belle arrived seconds later, she saw that Gaston had forced the Beast to the edge of the castle roof. "No!" Belle screamed.

The sound of Belle's voice snapped the Beast into action. He grabbed Gaston by the neck and dangled him over the edge of the roof.

"Let me go! I'll do anything!" Gaston pleaded.

Full of rage, the Beast hesitated for just a moment. Then he realized he was not really a beast at heart. He tossed Gaston safely back on to the balcony, and turned towards Belle, who had raced up the stairs to find him.

But just as the Beast moved to embrace Belle, Gaston pulled a long hunting knife from his boot...and stabbed the Beast in the back.

The Beast let out a howl of pain. Gaston took a frightened step backwards, tripped over the edge, and plunged from the roof.

But the Beast had been terribly wounded. Belle ran to his side and embraced him. "You came back," the Beast whispered. "At least I got to see you one last time."

"Don't talk like that. You'll be all right," Belle said, fighting back tears.

In the Beast's room, the last petal was about to drop from the rose.

"**N**o! Please don't leave me. I love you," Belle sobbed, leaning down to kiss him just as the last petal fell.

Magically, the Beast rose and changed back into his human form.

"Belle, it's me," said the Prince.

Belle rushed into the Prince's arms. As they kissed, magic filled the air. Soon Lumiere, Cogsworth, Mrs. Potts and Chip, and all the other enchanted objects were transformed back into their human forms.

That night, the castle was filled with love as Belle and the Prince danced and danced, barely able to take their eyes off each other. And the castle was once again filled with life.

Disney's

BROTHER

BEAR

In the days when ice still covered much of the earth and great herds of mammoth roamed free, three brothers lived together in a small village near the coast. Our story begins on the day of a special ceremony for the youngest brother, Kenai.

The villagers gathered around as Tanana the shaman presented Kenai with a special totem. "Kenai, I have been to the mountain where the lights touch the earth," said Tanana, "To become a man your actions must be guided by one thing: Your totem is…love." Then Tanana placed the bear totem around Kenai's neck.

"The bear of love?" Kenai frowned in disappointment.

"Let love guide your actions," said Tanana as she gazed at the wall of handprints. "And one day, you will place your mark next to those of your ancestors.

After the ceremony, Kenai and his brothers, Sitka, and Denahi, headed back to collect the fish they'd caught for this evening's feast. Years before, Sitka had received the eagle of guidance, and Denahi had received the wolf of wisdom. Kenai stopped abruptly. Up ahead, Denahi held the remains of Kenai's broken basket. A bear had torn into the basket full of fish and made off with it. Following the bear's tracks Kenai went into the woods alone to find the basket.

After Kenai had been gone for a long time, Sitka and Denahi heard a sharp cry ring out.

It was Kenai. They raced to find him and when they did, he wasn't alone. A huge grizzly bear loomed over him! Sitka helped Kenai while Denahi lunged at the great bear with his spear. But the bear swatted at Denahi and sent him flying across an icy glacier. While Kenai helped Denahi, Sitka tried his best to fight the grizzly, but the bear was too powerful for him.

The bear growled angrily and headed right for Kenai and Denahi. Sitka had to do something to save his brothers! He raised his spear in the air and plunged it down into a crack in the ice. The ground shook as the glacier split taking Sitka and the bear down with it into the freezing water below.

As they watched from the top of the cliff, Kenai and Denahi saw the bear emerge from the water…but not Sitka. Sitka had just saved his brothers lives but there was nothing they could do to save his.

Kenai grabbed two spears and threw one to Denahi. "We are going after the bear," he said. Denahi tried to stop him but Kenai set out alone to kill the monster that had taken his brother's life.

Kenai tracked the bear down in a rocky canyon. The bear charged. Roaring towards him, Kenai raised his spear towards the huge grizzly. The bear let out a great roar and then fell silent.

Then something amazing happened. Magical lights burst down from the skies turning into animal spirits and swirling around Kenai!

Kenai watched in amazement as a giant eagle swooped down to land next to him and then turned into Sitka. Before he could speak, Kenai felt a weird sensation washing over his body. Something very strange was happening! Kenai was lifted into the air and turned into the very creature he hated most: a bear!

Dazed, Kenai was lowered down on the ground, just as Sitka and the lights disappeared and it began to rain.

Meanwhile Denahi, who had been following his brother, finally caught up with him on the rocky plateau. His eyes widened as he saw a grizzly bear standing on his brother's clothes. Not realizing the bear was Kenai, Denahi thought the bear must have killed his younger brother. At that moment, a bolt of lightning ripped through the air, sending Kenai tumbling down the side of the cliff to the river below.

When Kenai opened his eyes the next morning, Tanana was leaning over him.

"Nana! You won't believe this!" exclaimed Kenai excited, "I was at the top of this huge rock and all of a sudden the spirits…"

But Tanana could only hear growls when he spoke to her.

"Kenai, I don't speak bear!" said Tanana.

Bear?

Kenai looked into the river at his reflection. "No no no!" he cried. He pulled at his new furry body and discovered a tail!

"AAAAAHHHHH!" cried Kenai.

Kenai ran around in a panic growling and roaring.

"Alright settle down Kenai," said Tanana, but Kenai wouldn't listen. Tanana took off her shoe and BONK! Kenai got a knock on the head.

"Listen to me! Sitka did this!" said Tanana.

"I can't help you. Take it up with your brother's spirit! If you want to change, go to the mountain where the lights touch the Earth."

"How do I get there?" asked Kenai. But Tanana had disappeared.

Kenai wandered through the forest alone when suddenly he heard voices. He was shocked, when he saw the voices were coming from two squirrels – and he could understand what they were saying!

"Hey! You just talked," said Kenai amused.

The squirrels took one look at the big bear and ran for their lives.

A little later, a flock of Geese flew by and Kenai could hear every word they said!

"Are we there yet?" a young goose asked his father.

"Don't make me turn this formation around!" said his father annoyed.

"**W**ait!" cried Kenai chasing after the geese, "I'm trying to find where the lights…!" But they were already long gone.

Behind some bushes nearby, two moose brothers were watching Kenai.

"What's he getting all worked up about!" said one of them named Tuke.

"Maybe the goose pooped on him eh?" said the one called Rutt. The moose laughed until they noticed that the bear had spotted them and was coming right towards them.

"How's it going bear?" said Tuke a little nervously.

"I'm not a bear…I hate bears," answered Kenai, still not sure quite what had happened to him.

"Well gee, you're one big beaver!" said Rutt.

"I'm NOT a beaver! I'm a man!" Kenai was getting frustrated. "I was transformed into a bear, " he said and added, "Magically."

Tuke mumbled to Rutt, "He's crazy!"

"I am not crazy!" said Kenai, who had heard every word they said.

"We understand," said Tuke, "We're not moose either. We're squirrels."

Knowing he would never get any help from these two, Kenai wandered off alone.

Life as a bear certainly wasn't easy. Suddenly Kenai's foot got caught in a trap and he flew up in the air.

"Aaaaaahhh!" he cried.

A bear cub named Koda popped out of the bushes. "Guess you didn't see the bear trap, huh? I saw it from a mile away," the small bear said.

As he struggled to get free, Kenai accidentally whacked his own head.
"Oooh, that was funny!" Koda giggled. "Do that again."
"Don't you have someplace to go?" asked Kenai annoyed.
"Yeah, the Salmon Run," said Koda, "How about this? I get you down—
then we go together?"

But Kenai was too stubborn, and he definitely did not want help from some silly bear cub! So Koda sat nearby and talked for hours, while Kenai struggled to free himself. Finally, Kenai was so exhausted that he agreed to go to the Salmon Run if Koda could free him. With that, Koda picked a peg out of the ground and Kenai crashed down to the earth.

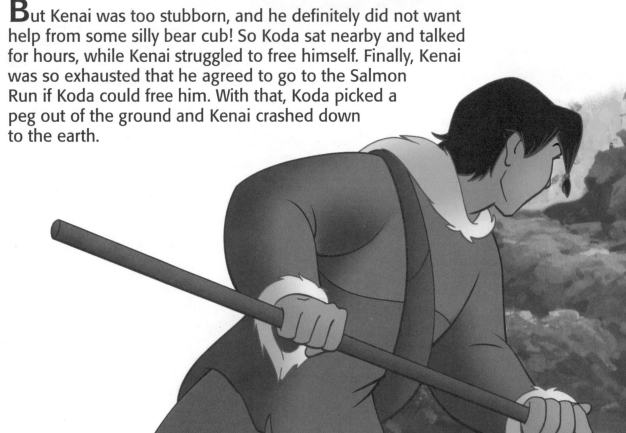

Suddenly Koda sniffed something in the air.

A hunter was coming towards them!

"Run!" cried Koda as he ran off into the woods frightened.

The hunter turned out to be none other than Denahi.

"Denahi, it's me--Kenai!" Kenai cried. But Denahi could not understand Kenai's growling. All he saw was the bear he thought had killed his brother.

Kenai escaped Denahi by hiding in the same ice cave where Koda was.

Confused and frustrated, Kenai backed out of his promise to go to the Salmon Run.

"I got separated from my mom," explained Koda. His only hope of finding her again was to go to the Salmon Run.

Still, Kenai wouldn't go.

"Please come," pleaded Koda, "Every night we watch the lights touch the mountain."

"You're kidding me!" said Kenai, brightening at the thought. Koda could lead him to the place where he could meet Sitka's spirit and turn back into a human! Reluctantly, Kenai agreed to go with the little cub.

Early the next morning, Kenai and Koda set out for the Salmon Run. Kenai soon found out that traveling with this little bear was not easy! Koda loved to entertain new friends, and play, and splash, and blow in the wind. While all Kenai wanted to do was get to the mountain. This cub who just wouldn't stop talking was slowing him down!

But after a while, Kenai found that he was actually enjoying himself. Maybe Koda wasn't so bad after all!

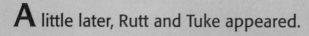

A little later, Rutt and Tuke appeared.

"There's this hunter followin' us," Rutt explained. The two moose thought Kenai could protect them from the hunter. But how could Kenai make sure that the hunter didn't follow their tracks? Suddenly, he had a brilliant idea…

Instead of walking on foot, they found a herd of mammoths and rode on their backs—just like Kenai used to do when he was still human. Neither Rutt, Tuke nor Koda had ever tried anything quite like it, but they had to admit that it would be hard for Denahi to follow them now.

That night, Koda gazed up at the lights in the northern sky and talked about the spirits.

"You know about the Great Spirits?" asked Kenai in amazement.

"Mom says the Spirits make magical changes in the world," said Koda.

"My brother Sitka is a Spirit," said Kenai, "if it wasn't for him, I wouldn't be here."

Koda looked up to the lights and said, "Thanks Sitka, If it weren't for you, I would have never met Kenai."

Koda snuggled up against Kenai and said, "You know, I always wanted a brother." And for the first time, Kenai let Koda sleep next to him.

After they got off the mammoths, Kenai and Koda left Rutt and Tuke behind. They soon came to an abandoned village with cave paintings. A painting of a hunter with a spear and a fierce bear reminded Kenai of what happened to his brother Sitka.

"Those monsters are really scary," Koda said as he came up from behind, "especially with those sticks." Kenai was surprised. He had always thought that the bears were the monsters. But Koda saw humans as monsters. Now, Kenai wasn't so sure what he felt anymore.

Soon Kenai and Koda came to a canyon with spurting geysers. Koda remembered that the Salmon Run was just on the other side of the geysers. Wanting to tease Kenai, Koda hid behind a rock and suddenly jumped out.

"Aaaah!" screamed Kenai.

"Scared you, didn't I?" laughed Koda.

But suddenly Koda stopped laughing. Thwack! A spear landed right next to Kenai, missing him by inches!

It was Denahi's spear! Quickly, Kenai grabbed Koda and rushed toward a log bridge. They were halfway over the bridge, when Denahi appeared and began to cut the log loose. Kenai tossed Koda up to safe ground and scrambled up the edge of the cliff just as the bridge collapsed. Denahi yelled in anguish as the bears got away.

"We made it!" cried Koda a little later as he looked out over the river filled with bears catching salmon. They had finally reached the Salmon Run. It felt great to be with all his old bear pals again. But sadly, Koda didn't find his mother among them.

Kenai was a bit reluctant and felt terrified around all these big bears. But they all welcomed Kenai with open arms. He was part of their family now!

And now Koda could show Kenai how much fun bear have!

Kenai was definitely happy to be close to the place, where the lights touch the Earth. Hopefully, he would be able to be turned back to his normal, human form.

That afternoon, the bears gathered around to hear stories of what had happened to them over the past year. When it was Koda's turn, he told about how he had lost his mother.

"Me and my mom were eating fish, when suddenly she pushes me into the bushes. Then out of the trees jumps a hunter!" said Koda. "Mom stands up and yells, 'Go away!' Mom smells more of them. So she runs out to stop them before they get to me. They were all around her, poking her with sticks."

Kenai couldn't believe what he was hearing. It was the story of the day his brother Sitka was killed by a bear…but now he knew it was also the story of a mother bear protecting her cub.

"Was she okay?" asked one of the bears.

"She got out of the water okay," said Koda, "But that's how we got separated. Right after that, I met Kenai."

Shocked, Kenai realized that the bear he had killed was none other than Koda's mother!

Kenai felt terrible. Because of him, his sweet little friend Koda had lost his mother forever. He had to run away.

It didn't take Koda long to find his friend. But he did not understand why Kenai seemed so sad. So Kenai explained to Koda the terrible thing he had done. Overwhelmed with emotion, Koda ran away from Kenai as fast as he could.

Kenai knew that no word he said could make up for what he'd done. Having nowhere else to go, he decided to climb the mountain to find the place, where the lights touch the Earth.

After a long and hard climb, Kenai reached the top.

"Sitka, are you there?" pleaded Kenai.

A strange figure moved towards Kenai. For a short while, it looked like Sitka … but it was Denahi! He charged at Kenai with his spear, ready to kill him. Kenai looked up at his brother with panic in his eyes. But Denahi could only see a bear beneath him, not his brother Kenai.

Suddenly Koda came charging in. Trying to protect his friend, Koda knocked into Denahi and ran off with his spear. Furious, Denahi took off after Koda.

"Leave him alone!" shouted Kenai as he raced over to protect Koda from his brother. At that very moment, there was a great flash of light.

From out of the light came the great eagle again. As he picked up Kenai off the ground, magical lights swirled around and turned Kenai back into a human. Denahi watched in utter amazement. The bear that he was trying so desperately to kill just moments before was his own brother Kenai!

The great eagle turned into the spirit of Sitka. Sitka had turned his brother into a bear so that Kenai could discover his gift of love. And now Kenai loved the bears that he once hated. He had protected Koda just as he would have done for his own brothers—willing to give his own life.

Kenai looked down at his human body in amazement. Then he spotted Koda, hiding behind a boulder, frightened and confused.

"Koda don't be afraid," said Kenai. "It's me."

Kenai wasn't sure he wanted to return to the village. Little Koda needed someone to protect him, just like Kenai's big brothers used to protect him.

"This isn't right. He needs me," Kenai said.

"It's alright Kenai," said Denahi, as he placed the bear totem around Kenai's neck. "No matter what you decide, you will always be my little brother."

And with a burst of swirling light beams, Sitka turned Kenai back into a bear.

Koda was delighted. He jumped into Kenai's furry arms. It was true that Koda had lost his mother, but he'd gained the best big brother a bear cub could ever have.

Then Kenai, Denahi and Koda looked up at the sky as Sitka turned into an eagle and flew back into the magical lights to join the Great Spirits.

Back in the village, Denahi told everyone Kenai's story. Tanana and the villagers celebrated how Kenai had learned to follow his totem.

Tanana made Denahi the new shaman and his first duty was to help his brother bear put his paw print on the great wall. Kenai smiled because now his paw print was surrounded by the human handprints of all his ancestors.

Now Kenai had three brothers: One an eagle spirit, Sitka; another the village shaman, Denahi; and the third, a little, very chatty bear cub named Koda.

Walt Disney's Cinderella

Once upon a time, in a faraway kingdom, there lived a young girl called Cinderella. She lived in a mansion with her Stepmother and two stepsisters, Anastasia and Drizella.

Cinderella was kind and lovely, while her stepsisters were selfish and ugly. Her Stepmother did not like Cinderella. She made her do all the housework and sleep in the attic.

But Cinderella always looked on the sunny side of life. She did her work cheerfully and made friends with the mice and birds for company.

Now, the King was hoping his son would marry and settle down. But how could he get his son to meet the right girl? Then he had a wonderful idea: He would have a ball in honor of his son. "And if all the eligible maidens in my kingdom just happened to be there…"

And so one morning the palace messenger appeared at the door of Cinderella's house with a special invitation.

"**A** ball! In honor of his highness the Prince…and, by royal command, every eligible maiden is to attend!" said the Stepmother as she read the invitation.

"Why, that means I can go, too," said Cinderella.

"Ha! Ha!" screeched the stepsisters. Then they began to mimic Cinderella at the ball. "I'd be honored, your highness…would you mind holding my broom?"

"Why not? After all, I'm still a member of the family," said Cinderella firmly.

"**W**ell, I see no reason why you can't go, if you get all your work done," said the Stepmother.

Cinderella's stepsisters were very upset. "Mother, do you realize what you just said?" they cried.

"Of course. I said *if,*" the Stepmother replied slyly.

"Oh, if!" said the stepsisters, grinning at each other.

And of course, Cinderella would have to find a suitable dress to wear to the ball. She hurried up to the attic to see what she could find.

In her room, Cinderella opened an old trunk and lifted out a dress with puffed sleeves. The mice watched her curiously. "Isn't it lovely?" she asked, looking in the mirror. "It was my mother's."

"Ess…butta…butta…dessa old," said a thin little mouse called Jaq.

"Oh, I'll fix that," said Cinderella. "I'll have to shorten the sleeves…I'll need a sash…"

Then the stepsisters called, "Cinderella!"

"Poor Cinderelly!" said the mice. "Every time she finds a minute…that's the time when they begin it."

"Oh, well…guess my dress'll have to wait," Cinderella said. Then she called down to her stepsisters, "All right, I'm coming!" She hurried out of the attic.

"You'll see!" squeaked Jaq. "They'll fix her. She'll never get her dress done."

Cinderella found her stepmother in the front hall with Anastasia and Drizella. They told her to wash the hall floor, even though she had cleaned it the day before.

"When you're through, and before you begin your regular chores, I have a few little things…" said the Stepmother.

Anastasia and Drizella also found some extra work for Cinderella to do. They wanted her to iron their ball gowns and curl their hair for the party—that is, after sweeping the fireplace, shining the pots and pans, and doing the laundry.

Cinderella had no choice but to do as they asked. All day long she worked, thinking sadly of her dress in the attic.

Meanwhile the mice and birds worked on Cinderella's dress.

Jaq and his new friend Gus scampered down to the stepsisters' room to see what they could find. The sisters were going through their cupboard.

"These old rags," sniffed Anastasia, dropping a sash on the floor.

Then Drizella tossed some beads she was tired of into a corner.

Gus and Jaq dragged the sash and beads up to the attic, right past Lucifer, the cat. When the other mice saw what Gus and Jaq had found, they cheered.

At the end of the day, Cinderella was still working with the stepsisters. Drizella made Cinderella help her try on one dress after another. None of them could make her look as pretty as Cinderella.

At last the sisters paraded downstairs, very pleased with themselves.

"I'm not going," sighed Cinderella as she climbed slowly to her attic. "Oh, well—what's a royal ball?" But when she opened the door her eyes lit up like stars.

"**S**urprise!" cried the mice and the birds. They couldn't wait to see her dressed in the pretty gown, and they were especially proud of all their work.

"Why, I never dreamed…it's such a surprise!" gasped Cinderella. "How can I ever…why…oh, thank you so much!" She could hardly believe that she would be able to go to the Prince's ball after all! She took off her old clothes and slipped into her new dress. She twirled around in front of the mirror. As she hurried out the door she blew a kiss to her little friends.

Downstairs, Drizella and Anastasia were being given a last minute check by their mother. The carriage was waiting for them outside.

The Stepmother was saying, "Now remember, when you are presented to his highness, be sure to—" She stopped and gasped. She couldn't believe her eyes. There, coming down the grand staircase, was Cinderella, prettier than ever and wearing a charming dress!

"Please! Wait for me!" called Cinderella. She ran down the stairs and held out her skirt. "Isn't it lovely? Do you like it? Do you?" she asked.

Drizella and Anastasia stared for a moment, horrified. "Mother, no!" they babbled, both talking at once. "She can't go! Do something!"

"Girls, girls!" said the Stepmother, waving her hand for silence. "After all, we did make a bargain." She turned to Cinderella. "Didn't we?"

Her eyes narrowed as she looked at Cinderella. "My, how very clever…these beads—they give it just the right touch, don't you think so, Drizella?"

"No, they do not!" screeched Drizella. "They…they…why, you little thief. Those are my beads. Give them here!" She snatched the beads from Cinderella's neck.

"Look! That's my sash! She's wearing my sash!" yelled Anastasia, ripping off the sash the mice had sewn on so carefully.

"No, stop!" wailed Cinderella, trying to defend herself. But Drizella and Anastasia tore at her dress, pulling off all of the frills and all of the bows. Soon Cinderella's beautiful gown was in tatters. It looked worse than her ordinary work clothes.

"Girls! That's quite enough," called the Stepmother curtly. "Hurry along now…both of you." And the three of them sailed through the great front door to the waiting carriage, leaving Cinderella alone and miserable in the hall.

Cinderella rushed into the garden and knelt by a stone bench, sobbing her heart out. It was so unfair! She'd always had faith in her dreams. And it had been her dearest wish to go to the ball, to wear a pretty dress, and to dance like other young girls!

"I can't believe, not anymore...there's nothing left to believe in," Cinderella moaned.

The mice watched miserably. Jaq and Gus knew that Cinderella's stepsisters didn't want her to go to the ball, but they could hardly believe that anyone could be so mean.

All the animals felt sad. Major, the old cart horse, and Bruno, the dog, tried to comfort Cinderella.

But something strange was twinkling in the air! Very soon, a kind-faced little lady was sitting on the bench, patting Cinderella's head and saying, "You can't go to the ball looking like that! But we'll have to hurry...."

"Why...then you must be—" said Cinderella.

"Your Fairy Godmother, of course!" said the stranger with a kindly smile.

Now let's see…," said the Fairy Godmother. With a few waves of her wand, she began making magic! She found a pumpkin for a coach and turned Cinderella's mice friends into horses. The horse, Major, became the Coachman, and Bruno, the family dog, turned into a Footman!

"**W**ell, hop in, my dear; we can't waste time."

"But…" Cinderella looked at her tatters.

"Now don't try to thank me…," said the Fairy Godmother.

"I mean, I do, but…don't you think my dress.…"

"Yes, yes, my dear, it's lovely—" Suddenly the Fairy Godmother's eyes opened wide. "Heavens, child, you can't go in that!"

The Fairy Godmother measured Cinderella with her wand. "What a gown this will be! Bibbidi, bobbidi, boo!" A shower of starlight whirled around Cinderella. As it melted away, there she stood in a sparkling ball gown.

"Oh!" gasped Cinderella, twirling around. "Did you ever see such a beautiful dress? And glass slippers! It's like a dream!"

"But like all dreams…well, I'm afraid this can't last forever. You'll have only till midnight and then…the spell will be broken.…"

"It's more than I ever hoped for!" said Cinderella, kissing the Fairy Godmother.

Away went Cinderella in her enchanted coach, racing beneath the starry sky toward the palace. Hundreds of people were gathered there for the ball. All the eligible maidens were being presented to the Prince. He didn't look very happy at all.

In the balcony above, the King and the Grand Duke watched. The King was feeling very grumpy. "Oh…the boy isn't cooperating," he growled.

"If I may say so, your majesty, I did try to warn you…," said the Grand Duke nervously.

"There must be at least one who'd make a suitable wife!" said the King.

Just then Drizella and Anastasia were being presented. The Prince rolled his eyes when he saw them. "I give up!" muttered the King.

But something had caught the Prince's eye. A beautiful young woman was wandering in the hall just outside the ballroom. She was by far the loveliest maiden at the palace that evening. Without so much as an "Excuse me," he strode out of the ballroom and went up to Cinderella.

The Prince bowed to her and without a word they walked slowly into the ballroom and began to dance.

The King was beside himself with joy. "Look at that!" he hissed, poking the Grand Duke. "Who is she?"

"I've never seen her before, sire," said the puzzled Grand Duke.

"Well, find out!" ordered the King.

Cinderella and the Prince waltzed 'round and 'round. They had eyes only for each other. Cinderella was sure that she was in love, as she gazed at her handsome partner.

All the guests were mystified. "Do we know her?" Drizella asked her sister.

"Well the Prince certainly seems to!" said Anastasia.

The Stepmother watched as the couple waltzed away towards the palace balcony. "There is something familiar about her," she said.

Cinderella and the Prince strolled into the palace garden and danced beneath the stars. But just as the Prince bent to kiss her, the palace clock began to chime midnight!

"I must go!" said Cinderella.

"Why?" replied the puzzled Prince. But Cinderella was already dashing away.

"Wait! I don't even know your name!" cried the Prince desperately.

But Cinderella didn't answer as she ran down the great staircase to her coach. She was in such a hurry that she left one of her glass slippers behind.

The Prince took the slipper to the Grand Duke. It was his only clue to finding the maiden with whom he had fallen in love.

To find its owner, the Grand Duke issued a proclamation that every maiden in the kingdom would try on the slipper.

Meanwhile Cinderella's coach was racing home. Ding! chimed the clock. Ding! Ding! As it reached the twelfth chime, the beautiful coach disappeared. Cinderella was left sitting on a pumpkin beside Major, Bruno, and the four mice.

"I forgot about everything, even the time," sighed Cinderella. "But it was so wonderful, and he was so handsome.... Oh, I'm sure that even the Prince himself couldn't have been more—"

"Your flipper, Cinderelly, your flipper!" squeaked Jaq.

There, on Cinderella's foot, twinkled the other slipper!

All night long the Grand Duke went from house to house, trying the glass slipper on all the sleepy maidens. The news of the search reached Cinderella's house. That's when Cinderella finally realized that her dance partner had been the Prince!

The Stepmother noticed Cinderella's dreamy expression and became very suspicious. She heard her humming music from the ball.

Cinderella raced up to her room to brush her hair. The Stepmother followed her. Before Cinderella could stop her, the wicked woman had locked the door!

Jaq and Gus watched in horror. "We've gotta get that key," whispered Jaq.

Meanwhile, the Grand Duke's coach rumbled into the courtyard. "Mother, Mother, the Grand Duke is here!" screeched Drizella and Anastasia, who had been watching at the window.

The Grand Duke walked slowly up the front stairs. A Footman carried the glass slipper on a velvet pillow.

"You honor our humble home," said the Stepmother. The stepsisters curtsied and giggled.

Anastasia and Drizella elbowed each other out of the way, each wanting to be the first to try on the glass slipper. Each sister tried to get her foot into the slipper. They pushed and squeezed as hard as they could, but it was no use.

Meanwhile, Jaq and Gus had scurried down to the drawing room where the Stepmother was busy talking to the Grand Duke. The brave little mice managed to steal the key from her pocket and had soon dragged it upstairs to Cinderella's attic to free her.

"You are the only ladies of the household, I presume…?" asked the weary Grand Duke.

"There's no one else," replied the Stepmother.

"Very well," said the Grand Duke, walking towards the door. "Good day, madam."

Suddenly he heard a sweet voice calling, "Please wait! May I try it on?" There on the staircase was Cinderella in her work clothes. The Grand Duke took one look at her feet and smiled. "Come, my child," he said, leading her to a chair. But the angry stepmother tripped the Footman as he carried over the slipper, and it smashed to pieces.

"Oh, no!" wailed the Grand Duke.

"But perhaps this would help," said Cinderella, taking a glass slipper from her pocket. "I have the other slipper."

As the mice cheered and the horrified sisters looked on, the Grand Duke put the slipper on Cinderella's foot. It was a perfect fit!

How happy the Grand Duke was! The King jumped for joy when he heard the news. And as for the Prince—well, in no time at all he married his lovely Cinderella, and they lived happily ever after!

Walt Disney's

ROBIN HOOD

Robin Hood lived with his Merry Men in Sherwood Forest. Some people said he was a hero. Others called him a bandit. Why? Because he robbed from the rich to give to the poor.

One day Robin and his friend Little John saw King Richard's golden carriage pass by. But the king was away at war. Instead, it was the king's wicked brother, Prince John, pretending to be king.

Seeing him there gave Robin an idea.

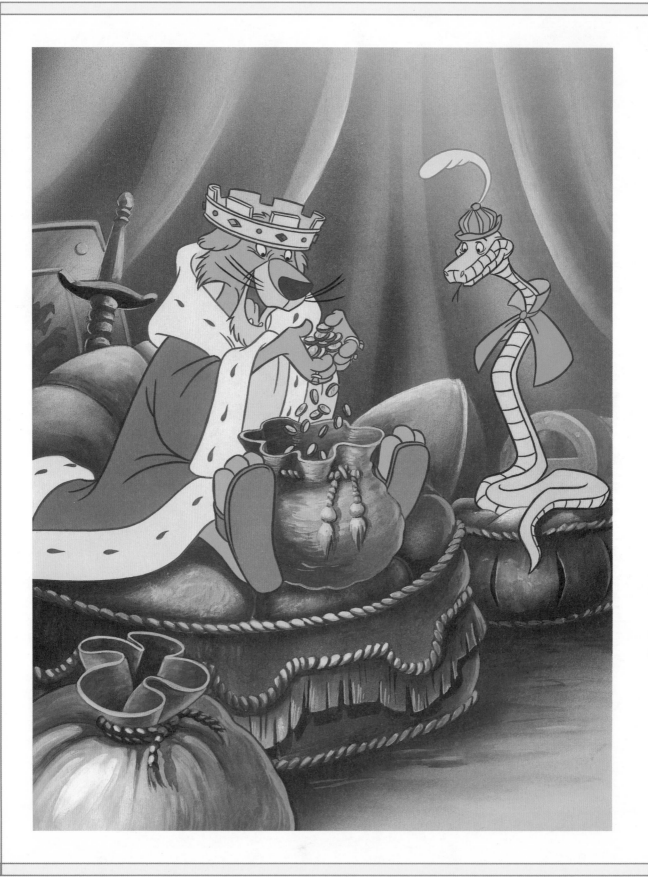

Robin and Little John disguised themselves as lady fortune-tellers. Then they raced after the royal coach. Robin cried, "Fortunes forecast, lucky charms!"

Inside the coach, Prince John had grown bored with counting his money. He was even more bored with Sir Hiss, the snake who served as his aide.

Sir Hiss spent his life trying to please the prince, but always managed to irritate him instead. Today, Sir Hiss had accidentally mentioned King Richard.

"Silly serpent!" Prince John snarled. "I told you never to mention my brother's name." Just then, Prince John saw the fortune-tellers and was ready for some amusement. Sir Hiss tried to warn him that the female fortune-tellers may be bandits. "You've hissed your last hisss…suspicious snake," Prince John scolded as he locked Sir Hiss in his basket.

Prince John ordered his coachmen to halt. "Step inside," he said to Robin and Little John.

Robin and Little John set up their crystal ball and put on a fine show for the prince. They knew exactly how to appeal to his greed.

Prince John gazed into the crystal ball, so charmed by the thought of riches that he paid no attention to the hissing sounds coming from the serpent's basket. Sir Hiss suspected a trick.

Sir Hiss hissed even louder when Robin grabbed hold of Sir John's huge sacks of gold and slid them quietly across the floor. The snake poked his long tail through a crack in the basket and tried to hang onto the gold, but he failed.

Robin leaped from the carriage with the gold, pausing only long enough to snatch the fancy ermine cloak right off Prince John's back.

Meanwhile, Little John managed to drain even more coins from a locked trunk, stealing them from right under the noses of the bearers who were supposed to be guarding them.

Then Little John loosened the wheels on the golden carriage.

When the prince finally realized that he had been tricked, he was enraged. "I've been robbed!" yelled the furious prince.

Robin Hood and Little John were already running away. Prince John ordered his guards to follow the thieves, but the carriage didn't get very far before its wheels fell off.

With his carriage disabled, Prince John had no hope of catching up with the thieves.

He had to watch helplessly, dressed only in his underwear, as Robin and Little John disappeared into Sherwood Forest, both of them loaded with jingling coins and jewels.

By the time Prince John returned to his castle, he was beside himself with rage.

He sent for his henchman, the wicked Sheriff of Nottingham. It was the Sheriff's job to collect taxes, and he was very good at it. He could sniff out gold wherever it was hidden.

For example, a poor blacksmith had tried to hide a few coins inside the cast on his broken leg, but the Sheriff simply grabbed the blacksmith's leg and shook out the gold. Even the good Friar Tuck couldn't stop him.

So when Prince John decided to take his revenge on Robin by raising the taxes yet again, the Sheriff was more than happy to help.

He headed for Skippy Bunny's house.

It was Skippy's birthday, and his sisters had saved all year to give him a shiny new gold coin.

"Happy birthday," the Sheriff said. With that, he snatched the coin, and was gone, leaving Skippy in tears.

Fortunately, Robin Hood showed up a few minutes later. Skippy stopped crying when he saw that Robin had brought not only more gold, but some special birthday gifts—a bow and arrows!

Absolutely everyone was excited about the Tournament of Golden Arrows. The best archer in the Kingdom would win a kiss from the lovely Maid Marian.

Robin loved Marian, even though he was afraid "such a high born lady of quality" would never marry an outlaw.

He decided to enter the tournament disguised as a stork. With luck, he would win Marian's kiss, and Prince John would never be the wiser.

Robin didn't know that Prince John had devised the tournament as a trap. Everyone knew that Robin Hood was the best archer in the land.

By the end of the day, only two archers were left—the stork and the Sheriff.

Then the stork fired his final arrow... a perfect bull's-eye!

Maid Marian was overjoyed, for she knew the stork must be none other than Robin Hood himself. And although Robin didn't know it, she was in love with him, too.

"Archer, I commend you, and because of your superior skill, you shall get what is coming to you," Prince John said. Then, as Robin bowed, Prince John sliced off the stork disguise with a swipe of his sword. "Seize him!" Prince John shouted.

The Sheriff led Robin away.

Robin knew that justice would only be done when King Richard returned. And so he said bravely, "Long live King Richard!"

Mention of the King's name made Prince John leap angrily from his throne. Then he felt someone holding a dagger to his back. It was Little John, disguised as a fat duke.

"Tell him to untie my buddy or I'll..." Little John said to him.

The prince had no choice. Robin and Little John had bested him again.

But the two outlaws still had to fight a messy battle with the guards before they made their escape back to Sherwood Forest. Robin Hood waved to his Maid Marian as he disappeared into the woods.

Back at the castle, Prince John was furious. And as usual, he was taking it out on Sir Hiss. This time he squeezed the snake until he turned green.

"Double the taxes," said the prince. "Triple the taxes! Squeeze every last drop out of those insolent...peasants."

So the prince raised taxes, and the Sheriff happily set out on his mission to make the poor people of Nottingham even poorer. Finally there was only one coin left in town—in the church collection box. The Sheriff took it.

"You thievin' scoundrel!" shouted Friar Tuck. He was so angry, he flew at the Sheriff with fists raised. That gave the Sheriff the excuse he had been waiting for. He threw the good Friar in prison.

At long last, Prince John was sure he had the perfect trap for Robin Hood. He was so excited that he pounded his fist on the table, frightening Sir Hiss.

"I'll use that fat Friar as bait to trap Robin Hood," said the prince. "When our elusive hero tries to rescue the corpulent cleric...my men will be ready."

Sir Hiss shook in fright.

News traveled fast, and it was not long before Robin heard about Friar Tuck's imprisonment. So he put on a new disguise and headed with Little John for Prince John's castle.

"Who goes there?" a guard called.

"Alms for the poor," Robin cried, dressed as a poor blind man. The guard was convinced Robin was a simple beggar, and let him pass.

Robin whipped off his beggar's disguise and dressed up like a guard. Then he and Little John crept into the castle to find the Sheriff.

The Sheriff was supposed to be on guard duty, but Robin found him sound asleep outside the cell door. Robin stretched out his hand for the keys, but the sound of footsteps made him dart back into the shadows.

Two guards marched past. Little John jumped the guards from behind, and soon had them trussed up like holiday turkeys.

Meanwhile, Robin grabbed the keys, and tossed them to his friend. "Now, you release Friar Tuck and the others, and I'll drop in on the royal treasury," he said.

Little John found the cell full of citizens who could not pay their taxes. Even the Bunny family was in chains. But no one was happier to see Little John than Friar Tuck.

In the royal bedchamber, all was quiet. Prince John was asleep, with his crown askew on his head. He was tightly clutching two bags of gold, dreaming of the day when all the money in the world would be his. More bags of gold were heaped around his bed and all around the room.

Sir Hiss was sound asleep in his cradle, his sharp eyes squeezed shut. Neither of them stirred as Robin crept silently into the room.

Watching them sleep, Robin Hood worked out a clever plan.

Carefully, Robin tied a long rope to the end of an arrow. Then he fired the arrow out the window, to the exact spot where he knew Little John, Friar Tuck, and the rest of his friends were waiting.

Very quietly, he attached Prince John's bags of gold to the rope, one by one, and slid them to his waiting friends.

As quickly as the bags of gold rolled in, Little John and Friar Tuck untied them from the rope while the freed prisoners waited anxiously.

Robin was quietly loading the last bags of gold right from under Prince John's nose when some tiny sound caused Sir Hiss's eyes to flash open.

Robin Hood barely had time to grab onto the rope himself, before Prince John and Sir Hiss flew into action. "They're getting away with my gold!" shouted Prince John.

But try as they might, Prince John and Sir Hiss could not reach Robin.

With his tail wrapped around Prince John's ankle and Prince John just barely holding on to his bed, Hiss stretched as far as he could. He managed to grab hold of the last sack of gold with his fangs. But the sack ripped, and the gold coins fell tumbling to the ground, to Prince John's horror.

Still, Prince John's cries woke the palace archers. They shot their arrows at Robin as Little John pulled his friend to safety.

Robin slid down the rope and into Little John's arms. But the friends were still in danger. The Sheriff was finally awake, and had called the guards into action.

"Keep going! Don't worry about me!" Robin said. He stayed behind to confront the Sheriff.

The Friar, Little John, and the freed prisoners ran for the palace drawbridge with the gold.

Meanwhile, Robin Hood climbed the walls of the castle tower, the wicked Sheriff and his band of archers hot on his heels.

"We got him now!" roared the evil Sheriff.

Then the Sheriff tripped and the fire from his torch touched the drapes, causing a fire!

The flames from the drapes spread throughout the castle. After a chase through the castle, Robin leapt from the tower into the moat just in time! He swam across the moat under a hail of arrows, and managed to escape into Sherwood Forest.

Meanwhile, Little John loaded the freed prisoners and the gold into a cart and sped across the castle drawbridge to safety.

Prince John's castle and his dreams were both in flames, and his fortune had been stolen. The only one upon whom he could exercise his fury was…Sir Hiss.

There was great joy in Sherwood Forest that night. Everyone cheered loudly for Robin Hood, even little Skippy Bunny.

A few days later, all the bells in the country rang to announce the return of King Richard. He would soon bring justice to the land!

Friar Tuck went to ask King Richard a very important question. Could Robin Hood marry the king's niece, the lovely Maid Marian?

"What?!!" King Richard cried. He wasn't sure at first, but then he accepted. "It appears that I now have an outlaw for an in-law. Not bad."

So shortly after that, Maid Marian's secret wish finally came true. She married her beloved Robin Hood, and they lived happily ever after.

And all of Nottingham celebrated with the happy couple at the wedding.

Disney's Aladdin

"Welcome to Agrabah, city of enchantment, of mystery, of delight . . . where things are never as they seem. This lamp for instance. It is no ordinary lamp. It once changed a young man's life. A young man, who, like this lamp, was more than he appeared. Come closer and I will tell you his tale."

It all began one night out in the vast Arabian desert, where a dark man with a dark purpose sat waiting in the moonlight. His name was Jafar, and he was Grand Vizier to the Sultan of Agrabah.

Suddenly, from the shadows, a second man appeared. "You have it, Gazeem?" growled Jafar.

Gazeem held up one half of a golden scarab. "I had to slit a few throats, but I got it." Jafar lunged for the scarab, but Gazeem pulled it away. "First where is the treasure you promised?"

"Trust me, my pungent friend," hissed Jafar as his parrot, Iago, ripped the scarab from Gazeem's hand. "You'll get what's coming to you."

Then, pulling the other half of the scarab out from his cloak, Jafar touched the two pieces together.

The scarab began to glow. Then it exploded into flight, leaving a gleaming path in its wake.

"Quickly!" yelled Jafar. "Follow the trail!"

The horsemen followed the magic scarab into the desert. At last it stopped its flight and buried itself in a mound of sand. And there, in the desert sand, a huge tiger head reared up.

"The Cave of Wonders!" exclaimed Jafar.

Jafar ordered Gazeem into the cave. "The treasure you find is yours, but the lamp is mine! Bring me the lamp!"

But as Gazeem stepped into the tiger's mouth, it roared. "Know this: Only one may enter here—one whose worth lies far within—a diamond in the rough!"

Then the Cave of Wonders sank back into the sand, swallowing up the unworthy Gazeem.

"I must find this diamond in the rough," said Jafar.

Early the next morning, in the marketplace of Agrabah, a young man took a loaf of bread.

"Stop, you street rat!" shouted the Sultan's guards.

But there was no stopping Aladdin (for that was his name). He and his sidekick, Abu, fled over rooftops, onto balconies, through open doorways, up steps, and down alleyways, always one step ahead of the guards.

Outwitted, the guards gave up. Aladdin and Abu sat down to eat. But when Aladdin saw others even hungrier than he, he couldn't help himself. He had to give them the bread.

So Aladdin and Abu returned to their humble quarters...tired, hungry, and poor as ever.

Gazing at the Sultan's palace, Aladdin made a promise to Abu. "One day we'll be rich, live in a palace, and never have any problems at all," he vowed.

Princess Jasmine would have laughed if she'd heard Aladdin say people in palaces have no troubles. She had plenty of them, starting with a law which said she had to marry a prince by her next birthday, which was only three days away.

Jasmine shared her worries with Rajah, her pet tiger. She was interrupted by the Sultan. "You've got to stop rejecting every prince who comes to call," he warned her.

"**F**ather, I hate being forced into this," replied Jasmine. "If I do marry, I want it to be for love. I've never done a thing on my own. I've never had real friends. I've never even been outside the palace walls!"

"But, Jasmine, you're a princess," protested her father.

"Maybe I don't want to be a princess anymore," Jasmine frowned. Maybe, she thought, just once, she'd like to fly free, like a bird.

Jasmine's refusal to take a husband had the Sultan in a sorry state. "I'm at my wit's end," he told his most trusted advisor, the evil Jafar.

"I have a solution," Jafar said coyly. "But it requires the use of the Mystique Blue Diamond that you wear."

"My ring?" protested the Sultan. "But...but..."

Jafar raised his cobra-headed staff and hypnotized the Sultan, hissing, "You will give me the Diamond."

"Whatever you need," the Sultan answered in a trance.

Grabbing the ring, Jafar stepped into a hidden passageway that led to his sorcerer's laboratory.

"Soon I will be Sultan, not that half-witted twit!" Jafar told Iago. "Once I find the one who can get us the lamp—the Diamond in the Rough!"

While Jafar plotted and planned, Jasmine acted on her dream. Disguising herself as a commoner, she made her way out of the palace. Only Rajah was there to see her escape.

"I'm sorry," she told him, "I can't stay here and have my life lived for me. I'll miss you." And she was gone.

Suddenly Jasmine found herself in a world she'd only dreamed about. Everywhere were crowds of people, new smells, new sights, new sounds. There were snake charmers, fire eaters, and hungry children.

Taking an apple from a stand, Jasmine handed it to a little boy. "Here you go." The princess smiled.

"You better be able to pay for that!" thundered the owner.

"Pay?" stammered Jasmine. "But I don't have any money."

"Thief!" screamed the vendor as he lunged at her. Suddenly a young man stepped out of the crowd and grabbed the vendor's arm. "Thank you, kind sir. I'm glad you found her," he said.

"You know this girl?" asked the shopkeeper.

"Sadly, yes. She is my crazy sister. Come along, sis," Aladdin said as he led Jasmine away. "Time to go see the doctor."

Meanwhile, in the tower above the palace, Jafar's secret laboratory crackled with lightning bolts and wicked plots. Using the Mystique Blue Diamond to raise the Sands of Time, Jafar commanded, "Show me the one who can enter the cave." The sands parted to reveal Aladdin.

"There he is," cooed Jafar, "my Diamond in the Rough. Shall we have the guards extend him an invitation to the palace?"

When Aladdin first spied Jasmine in the marketplace, a most peculiar thing had happened. His pulse began racing. His heart started pounding. He suddenly felt he had to know this girl and everything about her. "Where are you from?" asked Aladdin as he sat with Jasmine on his rooftop.

"What does it matter?" she replied. "I ran away and I am not going back."

As Jasmine and Aladdin sat and talked, the day grew dreamy, quiet, soft, romantic . . . at least until the palace guards pushed their way up the stairs.

"Here you are!" they bellowed.

"They're after me!" cried Jasmine and Aladdin together. "They're after you?" Jasmine and Aladdin said to each other.

Then there was no time for talk. Throwing Jasmine aside, the guards rushed at Aladdin. "It's the dungeon for you, boy!"

Throwing back her scarf, Jasmine declared, "Unhand him, by order of the Princess!"

"I would," said the shocked captain of the guards, "but my orders come from Jafar."

Once back in the palace, the Princess confronted Jafar.

"The guards took a boy from the market on your orders."

"The boy was a criminal."

"What was his crime?" asked Jasmine.

"Kidnapping the Princess," said Jafar.

"He didn't kidnap me. I ran away."

"Oh, dear," mocked Jafar. "Had I but known! Too bad the boy's sentence has already been carried out."

But Aladdin hadn't been sentenced to death—just to a cold, dark dungeon cell.

"A princess!" an astonished Aladdin told Abu. "What would she want with a street rat? She deserves a prince. I'm a fool."

"You're only a fool if you give up, boy." It was Jafar, disguised as an old prisoner. Now he told Aladdin, "There is a cave, boy—a cave of wonders, filled with treasures enough to impress even your princess."

Leading Aladdin and Abu out of the dungeon, the disguised Jafar brought them to the Cave of Wonders. "Bring me the lamp!" cried Jafar as the cave rose from the sand.

Carefully, Aladdin approached the monstrous tiger head as it roared, "Who disturbs my slumber?"

"It is I," said Aladdin.

"Proceed," thundered the voice of the cave.

Aladdin and Abu followed the steep steps down, down, down, until they found a huge chamber filled with mounds of treasure!

"Just a handful of this would make me richer than the Sultan!" exclaimed Aladdin.

But he knew better than to take it, for the tiger had warned, "Touch nothing but the lamp."

Oddly, though, as Aladdin and Abu explored the cave, something kept trying to get their attention. Abu saw it first—a richly-embroidered carpet playing hide and seek with him from behind a pile of gold coins.

"A magic carpet!" cried Aladdin when he spied it. "Come on out. We're not going to hurt you. Maybe you can help us. We're trying to find this lamp."

The carpet led Aladdin deeper and deeper into the cave.

At last, they came to a great underwater lake. In its center was a huge altar of rocks. And at its top, glowing in a radiant light, sat the lamp. One by one, Aladdin scaled the rocks until he stood before it.

"This is it, Abu?" asked Aladdin as he picked up an ordinary looking lamp. "This is what we came for?"

But Abu wasn't paying attention. His eyes were riveted on the hands of a statue holding a huge gem. As he lunged for it, the carpet tried to hold him back.

Aladdin shouted, "Abu! No!" But it was too late.

"Infidels!" thundered the voice of the cave. "You have touched forbidden treasures! Now you will never again see the light of day!"

Then the ground began to rumble and shake. The rock Aladdin stood upon collapsed, flinging him into the air. The carpet caught Aladdin just as the cave floor turned to molten rock. Grabbing Abu, the three of them headed for the mouth of the cave. But Aladdin was thrown from the carpet!

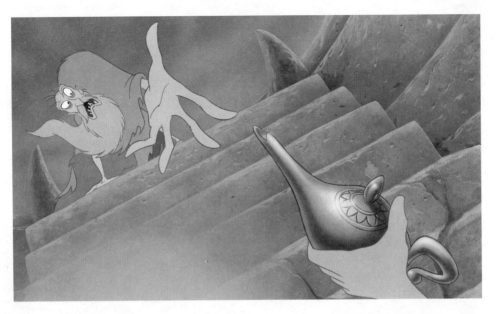

Struggling to hold onto the side of the crumbling cave, Aladdin begged Jafar for help.

"First give me the lamp!" said Jafar as he seized it from Aladdin. Then he drew a dagger from his cloak.

"What are you doing?" asked Aladdin in shock.

"Giving you your eternal reward!" crowed Jafar as he struck at Aladdin. But Abu grabbed Jafar's hand and bit down hard. Jafar pulled away in pain as Aladdin and Abu tumbled back into the cave.

"That two-faced son of a jackal!" exclaimed Aladdin as he sat trapped inside the cave. "Whoever he was, he's long gone with that lamp."

Abu just smiled. Then he pulled the lamp from inside his shirt and offered it to Aladdin.

"Why, you hairy little thief!" laughed Aladdin.

"It looks like a beat-up, worthless piece of junk," Aladdin said, turning the lamp over and over. "Wait—I think there's something written here. It's hard to make out." Aladdin rubbed the lamp. Sparks flew, smoke swirled, and suddenly, a genie appeared!

"Does it ever feel good to be out of there!" the Genie shouted. "Ten thousand years will give you such a crick in the neck!"

Then the Genie told Aladdin, "You get three wishes and ix-nay on the wishing for more wishes."

"Some all-powerful Genie," said Aladdin, winking at Abu. "You probably can't even get us out of this cave."

"Are you looking at me? Did you rub my lamp? Did you wake me up? Sit down and keep your hands inside the carpet! We're out of here!" The Genie took up Aladdin's challenge and they swooped out of the cave.

Meanwhile, at the palace, an angry Jasmine told her father about Aladdin. Even this great wrong didn't make the Sultan doubt Jafar. But Jasmine did.

"Some good will come from my being forced to marry," she told him. "When I am queen, I will have the power to get rid of you."

"Not if you become her husband," whispered Iago in Jafar's ear. "Then you become the Sultan!"

Aladdin had a very different idea about the man the princess should marry.

"Can you make me a prince?" he asked the Genie. It was done with the wave of a hand.

"Now for mode of transportation," said the Genie, eyeing Abu. "What better way to make your entrance into Agrabah than riding your very own elephant?"

Presto! Abu was transformed. "Talk about trunk space!" laughed the Genie.

"But we're not through," the Genie told Aladdin. "Hang onto your turban, kid."

Then he raised his hands once more. Sparks shot out. Trumpets called. Suddenly, an army of soldiers appeared, along with a parade of sword twirlers, and a harem of dancing girls all leading Aladdin, now Prince Ali, into town.

Aladdin bowed before the Sultan. "I have journeyed from afar to seek your daughter's hand," said the Prince.

"Prince Ali Ababwa, I'm delighted to meet you," said the Sultan.

But Jasmine was not so easily impressed. "How dare you!" she stormed at her father and Aladdin. "Standing around deciding my future. I am not some prize to be won."

"**W**hat am I going to do?" Aladdin asked the Genie. "Jasmine won't let me talk to her. I should have known I couldn't pull off this prince wish."

"Tell her the truth!" advised the Genie.

"No way! If Jasmine found out I was some crummy street rat, she'd laugh at me," Aladdin sighed.

That night, Aladdin did his best to impress Jasmine. But all she said was, "Leave me alone."

Saddened, Aladdin told her, "You're right. You aren't some prize to be won. You should be free to make your own choice." That did it.

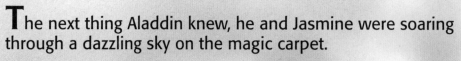

The next thing Aladdin knew, he and Jasmine were soaring through a dazzling sky on the magic carpet.

By the time Aladdin returned Jasmine to the palace, she knew the man she wanted to marry. "Goodnight, my prince," she whispered.

Floating back to Earth, Aladdin told himself, "For the first time in my life, things are starting to go right." That's when Jafar's men jumped him! "You've worn out your welcome, Prince Abooboo," threatened Jafar. Then tying up Aladdin and gagging him, they threw him into the sea!

Aladdin dropped like a stone! But as he sank into unconsciousness, the sand rubbed the lamp.

"It never fails," complained the Genie, "Get in the bath, there's a rub at the lamp." Then he saw Aladdin. "Al? Kid! Snap out of it. I can't help you unless you make a wish!"

But Aladdin was too far gone to reply. Shaking his head up and down, the Genie said, "I'll take that for a yes. Up scope." And he carried Aladdin to the surface.

Believing he'd rid the world of Prince Ali, Jafar hypnotized the Sultan into telling Jasmine, "I've chosen a husband for you. You will wed Jafar."

"Never!" she cried. "I choose Prince Ali."

"Prince Ali left," said Jafar.

"Check your crystal ball again, Jafar," said Aladdin as he entered the Sultan's throne room. "Tell them how you tried to kill me, Jafar."

"He's obviously lying," claimed Jafar, as he pulled away from the guards. Then, with a whoosh, he disappeared!

Safe in his secret laboratory, Jafar sent Iago to steal the magic lamp from Aladdin's room. With a single rub, the power of the Genie was Jafar's to control.

"I am your master now!" thundered Jafar. "I wish to rule on high as Sultan."

Instantly, the peaceful, sunny kingdom turned black as doom. Jafar was transformed into the Sultan. And as the people of Agrabah watched in horror, the genie reached down and plucked the palace up, up, up into the air.

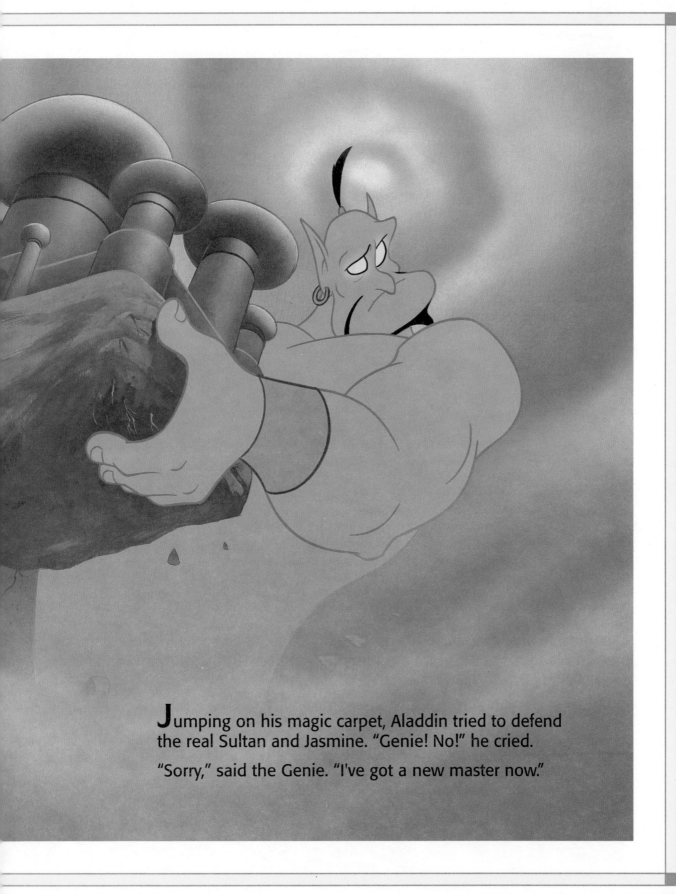

Jumping on his magic carpet, Aladdin tried to defend the real Sultan and Jasmine. "Genie! No!" he cried.

"Sorry," said the Genie. "I've got a new master now."

Sending sparks flying from his magic staff, Jafar started a whirlwind that pushed Aladdin and Abu into a tower of the palace and shot them to the very ends of the earth.

Chattering with the cold, Aladdin cradled the frozen Abu in his arms. "This is all my fault," said Aladdin as he began to walk through the high snow drifts. "Somehow I've got to go back and set things right."

Meanwhile, back in Agrabah, Jafar was doing his best to destroy the Sultan and Jasmine. It looked hopeless until Jasmine spotted Aladdin, who had made his way back on the magic carpet.

Determined to distract Jafar, Jasmine pulled his beard and whispered in his ear, "I never realized how incredibly handsome you are."

Aladdin saw his chance and hurled himself at Jafar. Lifting his staff, Jafar cried out, "How many times do I have to kill you, boy?" Then the wicked sorcerer surrounded himself with a wall of flames, and the lamp with a circle of swords.

"Afraid to fight me yourself, you cowardly snake?" taunted Aladdin.

"A snake, am I?" Jafar replied. Then, changing himself into a huge, gigantic snake, he turned his venom on Aladdin.

Striking out with his sword, Aladdin slashed at Jafar. Howling with pain, Jafar summoned up all of his strength and knocked the sword out of Aladdin's hand.

"You thought you could defeat the most powerful being on Earth?" hissed Jafar. "Without the Genie, you're nothing!"

We'll see about that, thought Aladdin. Then he called to Jafar, "The Genie has more power than you'll ever have! He gave you your power and he can take it away. You're still second best."

"I make my third wish," Jafar commanded the Genie. "I wish to be an all-powerful genie!" And it was done.

"The universe is mine to command!" cackled Jafar.

"Not so fast," said Aladdin. "Aren't you forgetting something? You wanted to be a genie—you got it. And everything that goes with it!" He picked up the magic lamp and imprisoned Jafar inside.

The ending was happy for everyone...except Aladdin. "Guess this is good-bye," he told the Princess.

"That stupid law," said Jasmine.

"Am I Sultan or am I Sultan?" said her father. "From this day forth, you shall marry whomever you deem worthy."

"I choose you . . . Aladdin," said a smiling Jasmine. And suddenly, for a street rat whose heart shone like a diamond, it felt like a whole new world.